GIRLS IN
LOVE

A SUMMER GIRLS NOVEL

Also by Hailey Abbott

SUMMER GIRLS

• • •

SUMMER BOYS SERIES

SUMMER BOYS

NEXT SUMMER

AFTER SUMMER

LAST SUMMER

• • •

GETTING LOST WITH BOYS

WAKING UP TO BOYS

THE SECRETS OF BOYS

THE PERFECT BOY

FORBIDDEN BOY

THE OTHER BOY

FLIRTING WITH BOYS

BOY CRAZY

GIRLS IN LOVE

A SUMMER GIRLS NOVEL

HAILEY ABBOTT

Point

New York   Toronto   London   Auckland
Sydney   Mexico City   New Delhi   Hong Kong

For Jon, with love

Library of Congress Cataloging-in-Publication Data
Abbott, Hailey.
    Girls in love : a Summer girls novel / Hailey Abbott.
        p. cm.
    Summary: Returning for another summer to the picturesque beach
town in Maine, teenaged cousins Jessica, Lara, and Greer face new
dating challenges.
    ISBN 978-0-545-10269-8 (alk. paper)
    (1. Dating (Social customs) — Fiction.   2. Cousins — Fiction.
3. Friendship — Fiction.   4. Beaches — Fiction.   5. Maine — Fiction.)
I. Title.
    PZ7.A149Gi 2010
    (Fic) — dc22

                                                    2009040300

                        ISBN 978-0-545-10269-8

alloy**entertainment**

Produced by Alloy Entertainment
151 West 26th Street
New York, NY 10001

SCHOLASTIC, POINT and associated logos are trademarks
and/or registered trademarks of Scholastic Inc.

12 11 10 9 8 7 6 5 4 3 2 1   10 11 12 13 14 15/0

Printed in the U.S.A.   40
First printing, May 2010

"Get your flip-flops off my pillow," Jessica yelped, giving her cousin Greer a playful shove. This sent a small avalanche of beauty products, the spoils of Greer's habitual pre-vacation Sephora trip, onto the bamboo floor of their bedroom.

Greer, who was from New York City and thus way too cool to be pushed around, shot Jessica a warning glance, but there was humor in her wide hazel eyes.

"These are not flip-flops," she corrected. "These are metallic thong sandals with hand-turned cork soles." She grinned. "By Dolce & Gabbana. Dolce & Gabbana probably hasn't made it to Ithaca, so I understand your mistake."

Jessica started to stick her tongue out at Greer but

decided against it. She was a year younger than Greer, but that didn't mean she had to act like it.

The three cousins — Jessica Tuttle, Greer Hallsey, and Lara Pressman — had only just arrived in the picturesque town of Pebble Beach, Maine, but they'd already laid claim to the biggest bedroom in the nicest of the three beach houses that the extended Tuttle family was renting. ("Because," Greer had reasoned sweetly, "if the three of us have to share a room, we're going to need *some* space." And Jessica's mom, Clare Tuttle, who liked to think she was in charge of the sprawling Tuttle family's sleeping arrangements, had, of course, agreed. No one could say no to Greer when she turned on what Jessica called her "Magical Charm Ray.")

Lara reached over the side of the bed and picked up one of the lipsticks that had rolled away during the commotion. "Mauve Minx?" she said doubtfully. "Who names these things anyway?"

Greer snatched it away playfully. "Mauve Minx sounds better than your Wet n Wild number 527," she countered.

Lara blinked her lovely blue eyes innocently. "Who, me? I stopped wearing that in sixth grade."

Jessica giggled, because she knew that wasn't true. Lara had plenty of fancy makeup, thanks to Greer's shopping tips, but she still had a soft spot for that drugstore pink. Plus it was only $1.99, and Lara was saving up to fix the Beetle convertible she'd bought last summer, which looked amazing but seemed to break down about once a month. Not to mention there were all those plane tickets Lara had bought to visit Jessica — and, more important, Jessica's older brother Drew — in Ithaca.

Jessica lay back against the soft bolster pillow and grinned. She was so glad to be back in Maine with her cousins; she'd been waiting for June all year, it seemed. Lara had flown in to Pebble Beach from Chicago, and Greer and her mother had made the trip from New York City in Greer's new convertible Lexus.

"Did I mention that my mother sang along to the radio the whole way here?" Greer sighed. She picked up a stray blush and dabbed a little on her cheeks. "Do you know what it's like to hear her try to channel Taylor Swift? It's, like, cruel and unusual punishment."

"At least you didn't have to fly coach from Chicago next to a guy with terrible B.O. and a deep desire to become your new best friend," Lara pointed out.

The two cousins proceeded to argue — good-naturedly of course — about whose trip to Pebble Beach was worse, and Jessica let her mind wander.

Though last year had had its share of misunderstandings and confusions — which was a nice way of saying "plenty of drama" — she knew that this year was going to be better. Maybe even the best summer yet. A lot of that had to do with Greer and Lara, but still more had to do with Connor Selden, the cute, sweet guy she'd fallen for last summer.

"What are you smiling about?" Lara asked, grabbing Jessica's toe and shaking it. "You need a pedi, by the way."

Jessica blushed. "I was thinking about Connor," she admitted.

"Connor!" Greer exclaimed, sounding uncharacteristically gushy. She'd always preferred him to his older brother, Liam, whom Jessica had liked first. "How is he? You guys are still together, huh? By the way, Lara's right about the pedi. I vote for a nice seashell pink."

Jessica nodded, ignoring the comments about her chipping toenail polish. "He came and visited once, and we talked almost every day. We even wrote letters!"

Jessica remembered Connor's visit to Ithaca — it had been so wonderful, but he'd had to leave much too soon! She had kept all of Connor's notes, though, and sometimes when she missed him she'd take them out and read them all in order. Her favorites were the ones where he talked about watching the sun set over the ocean, and how he always imagined he was watching it with her and holding her in his arms. It was so romantic, she almost couldn't believe her luck.

Lara raised her eyebrows. "Letters? You mean, not e-mail, but with real pen and paper? It must be true love."

Jessica blushed at this last word.

"Or maybe they don't have e-mail in Ithaca, either," Greer said drily. She seemed to think that New York was the only real city there was, and that everything else was some sort of backward village where people lived in grass huts and let their sheep graze in the public square.

"Very funny," Jessica said. "We're not a total cow town, you know. We do have Cornell, remember?"

Greer grinned slyly. "How could I forget? Cornell — and Cornell *guys*. I really ought to visit you more often."

Lara waved her hands over her head. "Hey, ladies, focus! We're talking about Connor and how much Jessica loooooooves him."

Greer laughed, but Jessica bit her lip, suddenly serious. Was it love? She wasn't sure what love felt like. Was love butterflies in your stomach? Was it feeling giddy just at the mention of a person's name? According to Britney Spears, love was "a state of grace, transcending time and space" — but Britney's music gave Jessica the dry heaves.

All she knew was that she felt incredibly close to Connor, especially after he visited. Over the time they'd been apart, she'd realized that she wanted to get even closer.

"I just —" She paused. "Um . . ."

"Spit it out, Jess," Greer commanded, pointing a

sharp-looking pencil at her. "This Bobbi Brown eyeliner can be used as a very effective weapon."

"Well," Jessica almost whispered, "you know how we only got together sort of at the end of the summer last year?" Her cousins nodded encouragingly. It had taken until August for Jessica to realize that Connor liked her, and that she liked him back. "Well, it meant that there hasn't been a lot of time for . . ." Jessica paused again. "A lot of time for . . ."

Lara frowned and pursed her little bow-shaped lips. "For *hanky-panky?*" she asked in her best schoolteacher voice. "Because you know what we say about *hanky-panky.*"

Jessica raised her eyebrows in confusion. "What?"

"The more the better!" Greer and Lara shrieked simultaneously.

Jessica was sure her cheeks were burning red. She wouldn't need blush for days at this rate. "You guys," she cried, "seriously!"

Her cousins immediately stopped cackling and looked at her, and Jessica was struck again at how gorgeous they both were: glamorous Greer with her statuesque figure and movie-star looks, and black-haired Lara with her pixie-ish beauty. She always felt like a tomboy next to them, even though they told her all the time that she was beautiful, too.

"Sort of like Heidi Klum," Greer always said, "if she were American instead of German."

Jessica hesitated, but she wanted them to know how she felt. "I mean, Connor and I have gotten really close in the past year. And now that we can finally be together, I want us to be even closer. Like, physically."

Greer looked up from the magazine she'd opened and stared at her. "Go on."

Jessica wanted to bury her face in her pillow but she made herself say it. "I want us to . . . I want him to be my first."

Lara's jaw dropped and she looked as if she might collapse onto the bamboo rug in shock.

Jessica felt her heart beating faster as she recalled the conversations she and Connor had had over the year. "We've — Connor and I have been talking about it. I don't even know whose idea it was first, but . . . we're both totally ready."

Greer smirked. "So little Jessi is growing up!"

Jessica shoved Greer again, this time with one athletic, very unpedicured foot. "Jessi*ca*. Or Jess, if you really can't be bothered to say all three syllables."

Lara struggled to look less surprised. "That's a big deal, Jess," she said. "Wow! I guess this summer is going to be different than last summer!" She walked over to one of the sleek, white laminate dressers and dumped in an armful of vintage scarves she'd taken out of her suitcase.

Jessica giggled as she flopped back down on Greer's big bed, gazing at the classic movie posters that Lara had brought all the way from Chicago and tacked to the room's clean, white walls. ("Bare is boring," Lara had said, pinning a *Roman Holiday* poster near the door. "Depends on what kind of bare you're talking about," Greer had countered, with a sly smile on her face.)

Jessica put her hands behind her head and sighed. "I sure hope it'll be different. I know that at least I won't be following Liam Selden around, waiting for him to notice me." She felt a tingle at the thought that she'd soon be spending all her time with Connor. "But what about you guys? What are you looking forward to? Maybe we should, like, write down our goals." Her mom always said writing something down was the best way to make it happen, which was why she stuck Post-it notes all over their house that said things like "Lose five pounds" and "Encourage children to do dishes more often."

Greer reached into her giant Chloe bag and pulled out a thick pad of paper and a glittery pink pen.

She could probably carry a whole typewriter in that bag, Jessica thought. Though Greer was really more of an iPhone type.

"Excellent idea," Greer said. She wrote Jessica's name at the top of a piece of paper and underneath it scribbled, *Lose virginity*.

"If my mom finds that, I will absolutely kill you," Jessica hissed, resisting the urge to snatch the paper from Greer's hands and burn it in one of the aromatherapy candles that dotted the room's bamboo shelves.

Greer laughed. "Don't worry. I'm *excellent* at hiding things." She wrote her own name next, thought for a minute, and then wrote, *Fall for a trustworthy guy*.

Jessica was startled. "What about Brady?" The son of the sailing club owner in Pebble Beach, Brady was handsome, sweet, and kind, and Greer had been head over heels for him last summer. Had he turned out to be a jerk somehow?

Greer brushed her silky brown hair away from her face and looked wistful. "He wasn't quite as perfect as I thought."

"Tell," Lara insisted. "Do we need to go to the sailing club and beat him up?"

Greer smiled at Lara's fiery look. "Fortunately not. He's spending the year sailing around Europe and the Mediterranean, working on the ship of some French billionaire or something. He said he couldn't pick a long-distance relationship over a chance to see the world. And you know what? I wouldn't, either." She straightened her shoulders. "But still. I want to find someone who'll stick around this time."

Jessica thought this sounded reasonable, though it was still a little surprising coming from Greer, who had broken about as many hearts as the beach had grains of sand. Usually Greer was the love-'em-and-leave-'em-weeping-in-the-dirt type. But then again, Jessica had been a total jock last summer, and now she wore high heels and dresses sometimes, so it seemed that people were capable of change.

"And you, Lara?" Jessica said, watching Greer write Lara's name on the paper, too.

Lara pursed her lips and looked thoughtful as she gazed up at the whirling ceiling fan. "I want to stop keeping secrets from people I love," she said.

Jessica was about to ask Lara to clarify her goal, but there was a knock on the door. She looked up in surprise, and suddenly Connor was bursting into the room, narrowly missing the pile of Greer's makeup that was still lying on the floor. He was already tanned from surfing, and his eyes were the color of the ocean on a stormy morning. Without even thinking, Jessica leapt off the bed and into his arms, and he picked her up and swung her around, planting a knee-weakening kiss on her lips. When he pulled away and she caught her breath, she saw her cousins grinning at her.

"Puppy love," Greer whispered, grinning, and this time Jessica *did* stick her tongue out at her.

Connor kept his arm tight around Jessica's shoulder. "Hey, girls, welcome back to the greatest town in all of North America. I'm going to steal Jessica away for a little while. But I'll see you tonight?"

Greer perked up. "At the bonfire?" There was always a bonfire to kick off the start of summer, complete with a keg, good music, and plenty of drool-worthy boys.

Connor shook his head. "No bonfire this year. It was getting old. All we did was sit around and watch a bunch of logs burn. Chace Warner's parents are in France for the summer, so he's having a party instead."

"But we don't know who that is," Lara pointed out.

Connor laughed. "Doesn't matter. There's always room on the guest list for three beautiful summer girls."

At that, the cousins grinned at one another.

Jessica glanced up at Connor, thrilled to be near him again after all those months apart. He looked taller, and he was definitely cuter. There was a bit of stubble on his cheek and she wanted to reach out and touch it with her fingertip. She didn't care about a party; she just wanted to be with him.

"We'll definitely come, then," Greer said. "And we'll raise a toast to our goals, girls, won't we?" She tucked the paper with their hopes for the summer into her purse and patted it protectively.

Jessica giggled and boldly slid her hand into Connor's back pocket, and she felt him kiss the top of her head. She was going to have a summer to remember. She was sure of it.

2

Greer was having an uncharacteristic desire for potato chips, so she pulled her hair into a tousled ponytail and went downstairs to the big chef's kitchen. She spied a bag of Lay's on the sleek granite counter and walked toward it, feeling slightly naughty. While normally she would never let something so greasy and, well, déclassé pass her lips, she decided that since it was the first day of vacation she would make an exception. She put a handful of chips on a plate and then began rooting around in the refrigerator for some celery and apple slices to counterbalance the grease.

As she extracted an apple from the crisper, she heard a loud, familiar laugh coming from the porch. Greer shut the refrigerator door and sighed. When she'd promised the Tuttles that she'd come back to Maine instead of yachting the Greek Islands or partying in the south of France like she'd done in previous summers, she had *not* expected that she'd have her mother tagging along with her.

She poured herself a glass of Evian (with a slice of lime, never lemon) and glumly reflected that had she known her mother would be part of the Pebble Beach crowd this year, she might have broken her promise to her cousins and taken that cute, young photographer up on his offer to drive her around Europe in a convertible Jaguar.

Her mother's giggle came again through the giant glass doors that led to the porch, and Greer heard a deeper, answering laugh. As in, a man's laugh — which meant that her mother had found some guy to flirt with, even though the ink on her divorce papers was hardly even dry. *That's it*, Greer said to herself. *I am* not *going to stand for this.* She tossed her head back and strutted right onto the porch, her expression so haughty it could have brought the more timid to tears. She was going to give her mother a piece of her mind. The words were already forming on her lips when her mother turned around and flashed the biggest smile Greer had practically ever seen on her.

"Darling!" her mother cried theatrically, holding her arms out from the end of the porch. An expansive, blue ocean stretched beyond her silhouette, the horizon dotted with white sails.

Greer was nearly distracted — she'd forgotten how

utterly beautiful it was here — but instead she scowled. "You look like someone just gave you a six-carat diamond necklace."

Cassandra Hallsey blinked innocently, as if she couldn't care less about diamonds, which was patently untrue. Sometimes Greer thought that if given the choice between her daughter and the Hope Diamond, Cassandra would take the latter. Greer's mother waved her outstretched hands, motioning Greer closer. "Darling, this is Michael. He is a lobsterman; isn't that fascinating? He came to drop off today's catch for our dinner."

Greer looked at the man who was standing on their porch in a faded T-shirt and wrinkled canvas pants. She saw that he was nearly speechless in the face of Cassandra's flirtations. Greer almost felt sorry for him. Cassandra Hallsey was a force of nature, and she looked as good as money could make her; she'd had her share of Botox and then some, and she'd taken private Pilates classes every day for nearly a decade.

Michael smiled at her, and Greer had to admit that he was cute, all suntanned and windblown. But still — he was half her mother's age, and he spent his days killing fish.

"Hi," she said coolly.

"He says that a yellowfin tuna can weigh up to four hundred fifty pounds! Isn't that incredible?" Cassandra gushed. She tossed her coppery hair over her shoulder.

Greer turned to her mother and realized, belatedly, that Cassandra was wearing Greer's own Tommy Hilfiger miniskirt. *The nerve!* Greer thought. Even if it did look pretty good on her — Cassandra had great legs, almost as good as Greer's — it was totally ridiculous. When did her mother turn into such a cougar?

Greer knew one thing for certain: She was *not* going to be competing for male attention with her mother. That was simply unacceptable.

Michael cleared his throat awkwardly. "I was telling this pretty lady here —"

"My *mother*," Greer interrupted.

"Um, yeah. I was telling her that yellowfins like to swim with dolphins, because dolphins are better at finding the little fish that yellowfins like to eat . . ." He trailed off uncertainly.

"Fascinating," Greer deadpanned. She reached out and grasped her mother's arm. "Don't you have a manicure appointment to schedule?"

Cassandra pulled away playfully, her green eyes sparkling. "First I have to pay this man for his delightful services."

Ugh, Greer thought. The way her mother said it made it sound like Michael had done a lot more than drop off the fish for the big Tuttle reunion dinner. *Gigolo much?*

16

Greer almost asked him. But she knew he was innocent — whatever was happening between the two of them was all her mother's doing.

Michael handed Cassandra the bill, and Cassandra took it from him gratefully, like it was a bouquet of roses. She leaned against the railing to sign it, making sure she gave the fisherman a good eyeful of her tanned, full bosom.

Michael stared — how could he not? Only a priest would be able to ignore those things.

When Cassandra returned the bill along with a stack of twenties, Greer half expected her mother to give him a kiss. But instead she gave a playful wave and a big, still-beautiful smile. "Don't be a stranger," Cassandra called as Michael headed down the steps to the beach.

Greer waited until he was out of earshot. She took a sip of her Evian and said coolly, "You're wearing my skirt."

Cassandra turned to her, her face a mask of innocence. "Well, it fits me so perfectly. How many mothers do you know who can fit into a size 2?"

Greer sighed. "That's beside the point. It's my skirt, and you shouldn't have taken it." *And you really shouldn't be wearing it at your age*, Greer thought. But she kept her mouth shut. Because in truth, she felt a little sorry for Cassandra. Ever since her marriage ended (which had come after years of separations and threats of divorce), Greer's mother had been at loose ends. Meanwhile her dad was off in Ibiza with a girl barely older than Greer. She shuddered at the thought.

Greer steeled herself to tell her mother the hard truth. She couldn't tell her dad not to wear a Speedo and chase girls half his age because he was on the other side of the world. But her mother was right here, on the big, cedar deck, and Greer was going to give her a piece of her mind. "You really shouldn't throw yourself at men like that," Greer asserted. Her mother only smiled, so Greer went on. "Act your age, Mom. And I mean the age you really are, not the age you tell everyone you are." There. She'd said it. It was mean, maybe, but it had to be done.

Cassandra reached for a bottle of champagne that was chilling in a silver ice bucket and popped the cork on it loudly. As she poured herself a glass of the golden liquid, she looked right into her daughter's hazel eyes. "Look," she said. "I've been miserable for the last six months. I've come to the beach to have some fun. And I'm going to have it, whether you like it or not."

Greer sighed. "So you're going to start drinking in the afternoon?"

Cassandra shook her head. "Only today, darling. It's our first day — a special occasion!" Cassandra smiled mischievously. "Summer is for fun, darling. And doesn't fun mean boys?"

Greer gazed out through the waving beach grass to the golden sand and the blue ocean beyond them. As much as she hated to admit it, Cassandra had a point. Greer just hoped she could get to the boys before her mother did.

Lara squinted into the mirror in the big bathroom she was sharing with Greer and Jessica for the summer. On the white, marble surface that surrounded the two deep sinks, Lara had spread out all the makeup she'd brought with her from Chicago. She held two blushes up, one to each cheek, and tried to decide which one looked more appropriate for that sun-kissed, beachy look. Not that she was sun-kissed at all yet; she was still pale from spending her days in the library, studying for finals. After staring confusedly at her cheeks for about five minutes, she put down the blushes and picked up a mineral bronzer, hoping that it would bring some color to her smooth, ivory skin.

She felt a little silly, honestly. Normally she was a lip-gloss-and-a-swipe-of-mascara kind of girl. She spent her time shopping for funky vintage dresses and jewelry from the sixties like Bakelite bracelets and beaded necklaces, not applying layers of makeup in front of a bathroom vanity. But she wanted to make sure she looked her best at dinner tonight, because it would be the first time she'd seen Drew in a month — and the first time she'd talked to him in three weeks, ever since their phone fight.

Drew and Lara had met last summer when they both got jobs waiting tables at Ahoy Grill. Their attraction had been immediate — after their job interview, they'd had the best spontaneous date ever — but then later that night, much to their mutual horror, they'd learned that they were step-cousins. That had been a *very* awkward moment, Lara remembered. And many more awkward moments had followed as they'd tried to ignore their feelings for each other.

When they couldn't ignore them any longer, there'd been the problem of keeping their relationship a secret. Because as nice and understanding as the Tuttle family was, Lara didn't think they were ready to embrace the whole cousins-as-lovers kind of thing. And she didn't want to do anything to jeopardize her mother's happiness with her new husband, Mike Tuttle. After half a dozen failed marriages, Lonnie Pressman-Tuttle was finally in a relationship that seemed to be working. And for that, Lara was extremely grateful. She'd spent enough nights sitting on the couch with her mother, watching bad Chevy Chase movies and eating Häagen Dazs out of the container, as Lonnie moaned about her latest romantic failure.

Lara picked up the Wet n Wild lipstick she told Greer and Jessica she didn't own anymore and put some on her lips. She made a kissy face, decided it looked too pink, and wiped if off again. She considered calling Greer into the bathroom for assistance, but then sighed and went back to work, shuffling through the metal tubes and plastic cases marked Stila, M·A·C, and L'Oréal.

She'd seen Drew often during the school year by flying to Ithaca over holidays and vacations. She'd told her mother that she wanted to visit Jessica, and Lonnie was more than happy to encourage a good relationship between her daughter and her daughter's new cousin. Of course, Lara thought with a smile, just *which* cousin and what *sort* of relationship was blossoming — well, what Lonnie didn't know wouldn't kill her. Anyway, Jessica knew about Drew and Lara, and, after a brief period of disgust and annoyance ("My own brother?" Jessica had wailed. "How could you not have told me?"), she had given the relationship her blessing. And she was always happy to meet Lara at the airport, right beside Drew, who stood there tall and slender, with appealingly shaggy hair, clutching a bouquet of peonies, her favorite.

Drew's parents didn't suspect anything because Lara slept on the air mattress in Jessica's room. Lara and Drew carefully planned their alone time around when his parents would be at work or out for dinner, and they managed to sneak in some pretty magical moments.

The last time Lara had visited, she and Drew had walked along the shore as the sun set over one of the Finger Lakes, turning the water pink and orange. Drew brought her hand to his mouth and kissed it, which made Lara giggle. "It's like we're in some cheesy romance movie or something," she said. "I mean, look at this sunset; it's so bright it looks totally fake. Like Brad Pitt should be riding off into it with Angelina Jolie or something."

Drew smiled. "Go ahead and laugh," he said. "*I'm* not afraid of romance."

"You are, too," she said, poking him in the ribs. "You're, like, allergic to it."

As if to prove her wrong, he kissed her then, gently at first, and then more insistently, and suddenly she'd felt breathless. Her mood became more serious.

"I think we should tell everyone," she whispered when he pulled away, "about us."

Immediately Drew frowned, and his emerald eyes seemed to go dark. "I don't think that's a good idea."

Disappointment welled up in her — disappointment and confusion. What was the big deal? They weren't related by blood! And if Jessica could handle the truth, Lara was pretty sure everyone else would be able to, too. She'd only met the rest of the Tuttles last summer, but they seemed like reasonable people.

Lara had reached out to touch him arm. "But Drew —"

He shook his head and smiled gently. "Not yet," he interrupted. "Let's just be a little patient." Then he kissed her again, and the sweetness of his lips made her forget about her request for a while.

That trip had ended on a good note. But the last phone call they'd had — well, that hadn't gone so great. She'd pressed Drew again to tell his family about their relationship, and he had responded by clamming up. The silence on the other end of the line was deafening.

After a while she couldn't stand it. She was annoyed and she let herself sound like it. "What, so you're just planning on keeping this a secret for the rest of our lives?"

She could hear Drew inhale and then slowly exhale. "No one said anything about the rest of our lives, Lara," he said softly.

Tears sprung immediately to her eyes, and rather than let him hear her cry, she hung up the phone.

Drew had called her back the next day, apologetic and sweet. He said that long-distance relationships were complicated ("Duh," she whispered), and then he suggested that they both think hard about what they wanted.

She knew what she wanted — him! — but she didn't say it, not then. She wanted Drew to say that he wanted her first. The problem was, he hadn't; after that conversation, he never called back. And though Lara was normally the type to take the relationship bull by its emotional horns, she was too hurt to call him. So while she waited for her phone to ring, three whole weeks had gone by, and here it was, mid-June, and they still hadn't talked.

Lara wasn't an idiot. She was pretty sure this was Drew's way of breaking up with her. Either that or they were in the longest fight they'd ever been in. (And practically the *only* fight they'd ever been in.) She was mad at Drew, without a doubt, but she still missed him terribly. She was anxious for his arrival, even if she'd have to keep her true feelings about him a secret from everyone but Jessica and Greer.

That was why it was so important for her to look good. She was hoping that Drew would fall for her all over again, and that he'd be so apologetic about his behavior that he'd leap up out of the deck chair overlooking the Maine ocean and dash over and sweep her up in his arms. She figured that she could forgive him pretty quickly if that was how it played out.

After another half an hour of preening, Lara was ready to go. She gave herself one last look in the mirror. The bronzer had given her a healthy glow, and the peachy blush just about screamed "sun-kissed." She'd put some black mascara and a dab of gold eye shadow on, which made her blue eyes seem electric. She straightened her shirt — a sweet little vintage peasant number she'd picked up at a boutique in Wicker Park — and then made her way downstairs.

The big, white kitchen and the giant, modern living room were empty. Everyone must be on the deck enjoying the ocean air, Lara thought. Her heart hammering, she put the tiniest of smiles on her face and walked expectantly out the great glass doors.

The breeze, cool and salty, blew her short, dark hair back and ruffled the lace on her blouse. She breathed deeply, thrilled to be back in Pebble Beach, as she scanned the porch for the one person she most wanted to see.

She spotted Greer and Jessica nibbling on crudités in the corner. To their left were Uncle Carr and her new stepdad, Mike, who were standing over the grill and arguing about how long the swordfish ought to be cooked. Her mother was laughing with Aunt Trudy, who was wearing a ridiculous pink sun hat. The whole clan was there, basking in the afternoon sunlight — everyone, that is, but Drew and his older brother, Jordan.

Lara fought a sinking feeling in her stomach as she walked over to her aunt Clare. "Looks like the gang's all here. But where's Drew?" she asked as casually as she could.

Clare took a sip of her rosé and smiled brightly. "Oh, he and his brother decided that they're going to be counselors at that camp they used to go to in Vermont. You know boys — you think they're going to do one thing and the next minute they do another."

Lara was so surprised that she couldn't even respond. Drew — *gone for the summer*? What about the plans they'd made — before they broke up? They were supposed to work at Ahoy Grill again together, and go sailing, and they were going to walk along the beach holding hands beneath the stars. And they were going to make out in the hot tub overlooking the ocean and go see rock shows in town and . . . and . . .

"What's the matter, dear?" Clare asked gently.

Lara looked up at her and tried to smile. She couldn't believe that she was only finding out about Drew's plans now. Why hadn't Jessica said anything? She shook her head confusedly at her aunt. "Oh, n-nothing," she stammered. "I just have a headache all of a sudden. I think I'm going to go sit down."

Dazed, she made her way over to Jessica and Greer.

"Hi, cuz!" Jessica cried, then bit into a carrot. Her T-shirt had GAP in big blue letters and a little piece of carrot on it that she'd apparently failed to get in her mouth.

Lara absolutely did *not* want them to know she was upset. She hated looking vulnerable even more than she hated clowns, snakes, and people who drove Hummers. She put on a brave face and sat down next to them. "So it's just us girls this summer," she said, keeping her voice casual and light. "No big brothers to slow you down, right, Jessica?"

Jessica smiled. "I know! I'll miss them, won't you? It'll be so different."

Lara tossed her head and pulled her Ray-Ban wayfarers down over her eyes. She realized that Jessica must have assumed she already knew about Drew's plans — which frankly was not an unreasonable assumption.

But he *hadn't* told her. He hadn't called her back, and he hadn't told her that he wasn't coming to Pebble Beach. Lara felt her heart squeeze. There was no denying it now, no hoping or wishing for another outcome. It *was* really and truly over with Drew before it had even really begun.

Lara refused to get mopey about it.

She snuck a beer out of the cooler and poured some into a blue plastic cup. "You're right it's going to be different," she announced firmly. "Different in a better way. Right, ladies?" At that, she raised her glass and drained it, as Greer laughed and Jessica clapped.

She put the cup down and wiped her mouth defiantly. She was spending the summer in a gorgeous Maine beach town and she was definitely single. "Let the party begin!"

4

Greer lingered by the pool at Chace Warner's house, gazing at the masses of people welcoming the summer season with stiff cocktails and shrimp on skewers. She saw a few of the boys she'd met last year, as well as plenty of fresh faces to pique her curiosity. As she leaned back in a lounge chair and crossed one long, tanned leg over the other (she'd made sure to get a base tan at the CLAY spa before arriving in Maine), she was pleased to see that there was no shortage of cute members of the male species. She saw one guy with a Yale T-shirt give her gams an appreciative look. She smirked to herself and took a sip of beer. Boys were so predictable.

Over in the far corner of the vast lawn, Jessica and Connor were getting reacquainted, an activity which, as far as Greer could tell, involved more kissing than talking. Not that she blamed Jessica! It was a beautiful June night in a beautiful beach town — it was the kind of night just *made* for making out.

Peering over the rim of her glass, she inspected her fellow partygoers more closely. Surely there was *someone* here worth kissing, she thought. Chace Warner had certainly wanted to kiss her, she reflected, smiling faintly. The Dartmouth sophomore responsible for the party had casually mentioned to Greer that he was single, rich, and looking for a girlfriend — all within five minutes of her arrival — but Greer had coolly brushed him off. She preferred come-ons that had at least a *touch* of subtlety. After all, Chace seemed to be talking to her boobs the whole time. And though Greer's boobs, cradled in their black Victoria's Secret push-up bra, were truly impressive, they were not very good conversationalists, which was why Greer objected when men talked at them like that.

Speaking of conversations, she knew she ought to be making some with the other people at the party but she preferred to remain aloof. This way she could focus on her own thoughts.

Thoughts like how, against her will, she still missed Brady. After so many misunderstandings last summer, it seemed as though they'd finally figured things out. They both cared for each other enough to try to make it work long distance: Greer had flown to Maine in October, and then they spent New Year's together in Manhattan. Instead of going out to a club (Brady claimed that clubs were too loud), they watched the ball drop on a flat-screen TV at the Fifth Avenue penthouse of one of Greer's classmates, and they kissed at midnight, drunk on champagne and each other.

Then suddenly he got the offer to captain some oil magnate's boat around the Greek Islands, and he jumped at the chance. And, as luck would have it, his ex-girlfriend, whom Greer naturally couldn't stand, was invited along as second-in-command.

"I hope they're seasick the entire three months," Greer whispered to herself. Or maybe, she thought, smiling slightly, Brady would get sick of that ex of his and toss her overboard in a shark-infested cove.

Imagining the Evil Ex's legs being gnawed off by a couple of hungry reef sharks made Greer feel a little better. And she knew that soon enough, she'd be feeling pretty great. After all, there were plenty of boys in Pebble Beach to help her forget Brady, weren't there?

As if on cue, the DJ that Chace Warner had hired began to play a techno version of The Marvelettes' "Too Many Fish in the Sea," and several of the guests began to get down on the dance floor that had been constructed over the shallow end of the pool. From one of the upper-story windows of Chace's Greek Revival mansion (an ostentatious new construction set on a hill overlooking the serene bay), some-one waved a pair of girls' underpants like a flag. *Tacky*, Greer thought. *Highly tacky.*

"Is this seat taken?" The voice was deep and sexy, and Greer looked up to see a tall guy with black hair and ice blue eyes gazing down at her like she was edible.

It was as if an invisible fairy godmother had suddenly created Greer's ideal man with a wave of her wand. Greer raised her eyebrows slightly and gave him a closer look. He wore a pair of dark-rinsed jeans and a white Oxford rolled at the sleeves, which hung, untucked and unbut-toned, over a gray T-shirt. His arms were muscular and tan, and she thought she could see the shadow of six-pack abs under his shirt.

She gave him a slow, sultry smile. "Now it is," she said, patting the chair beside her.

He had a pitcher of beer in his hand, and he refilled both their glasses as he settled in next to her. "My name's Hunter."

She eyed him over her drink, liking what she saw more and more every minute. "I'm Greer."

He nodded, looking very interested in learning more about her. "Are you a friend of Chace's?"

"He *wishes* I was." She smiled, knowing it would take the sting out of her words.

Hunter laughed and took a drink of beer. "What, you didn't fall for his charms? Because Chace likes to think of himself as a ladies' man."

Greer spotted Chace on the other side of the pool, chatting with two girls who looked about fourteen years old. "For a ladies' man, he seems to pay a lot of attention to *children*. Do those two come with a babysitter? Also, what's with the shorts he's wearing? Doesn't he know that only old men wear madras?"

Smiling, Hunter held up his hand. "Whoa, give the guy a break. That's his beer you're drinking."

"If it was better beer, maybe I'd be nicer," Greer said teasingly. "It tastes like skunked Bud."

Hunter grinned even bigger, locking his ice blue eyes on hers. "You're a spitfire, aren't you?"

She tossed her hair, which was positively gleaming thanks to the hot oil pack she'd used earlier. "I'm just calling it like I see it."

"Those gorgeous eyes of yours are pretty sharp." His voice was playful, suggestive.

He's so obviously a player, Greer thought. Hunter was hot and he knew it — anyone could see that. Which meant that, according to her official goal for the summer, he was not the kind of guy she ought to be talking to. But he was so handsome, with his long, black eyelashes and high cheekbones. *What's the harm?* she asked herself. It was the first night of the summer. Wasn't she allowed to break her own rule just once? An early misstep, after all, would leave plenty of room for improvement.

She reached out and touched his arm lightly. "Why don't you show me around your friend's house," she suggested.

Hunter looked carefully at her to make sure she wasn't teasing him, and then he grinned and took her hand. He walked her into the house, through the huge living room to a dark, wood-paneled library. He pointed to the bookshelves and began to say something about the architecture of the house, or maybe about the number of volumes Chace's parents had, but Greer wasn't really paying any attention. She was too busy looking for a soft couch for them to collapse onto.

They left the library when a group of four tipsy people came in to play cards, and they were chased from the sunroom by a slobbering, white dog who was intent on humping Hunter's leg. But eventually they found themselves upstairs, in a bedroom with a four-poster bed covered with a silky, gray comforter.

Hunter looked around. "I think this is where Chace's grandma stays when she visits."

Greer scoffed. "Wow, you really know how to be romantic, don't you?"

Hunter took a step closer to her and she felt the warmth of his skin, even though they weren't touching yet. "Actually I do," he said softly, reaching out to run a hand along her cheek.

She smiled. "The bedspread matches your shirt. Why don't you go lay down on it," she whispered.

Hunter narrowed his blue eyes, as if he didn't think she was serious.

Greer laughed and gently shoved him toward the bed, feeling the swell of his muscles under her palms. She wondered who he thought he was fooling with the innocent act. Certainly not her.

They collapsed onto the quilt, and Greer wrapped her arms around his warm, broad shoulders. He pressed his mouth against hers, and Greer felt that old familiar feeling, like she was at the very top of a roller-coaster hill and about to plunge down.

He kissed her cheeks and then her neck, and she arched into him.

"It's nice to meet you," she said playfully, kicking off her shoes. "You're making me feel very welcome here in Maine."

Hunter pulled his shirt over his head, and she reached up to touch his tanned, defined muscles. "I think we might become very good friends," he whispered.

Greer shivered with anticipation as he bent down to kiss

her again, and then she closed her eyes and let herself do what she'd said she wouldn't, and it was wonderful.

After a serious make-out session, they emerged from the bedroom with their arms around each other and their lips swollen from kissing. At the end of the long hallway, a dark figure came stumbling toward them. As the figure neared, they realized that it was their host, who was looking almost green in the face.

"You going to pray to the porcelain goddess, buddy?" Hunter called out to Chace, and Greer giggled.

Her whole body felt warm and tingly, and even though she told herself it was all an act on Hunter's part, she loved the feeling of his arm around her shoulders.

Chace waved at them as he barreled past. "Puke and rally!" he cried. "Never let the tequila get you down!"

"That's my boy," Hunter replied, laughing. "See you back downstairs."

"Gross," Greer whispered, but neither Chace nor Hunter heard her.

Greer and Hunter made their way back to the party, and as they approached the pool, Greer disentangled herself from Hunter. She didn't want to, but rules were rules. You could break them once, but then you had to stick to them. *Trustworthy guy*, she reminded herself. *Find a trustworthy guy.* To meet that goal meant she had to say good-bye to Hunter, no matter how much she wanted to snuggle up to him in front of the crackling fire someone had started in the fire pit.

"I'm going to go home now," she said, stepping away from him.

Hunter turned to her in surprise. "Don't you want to hang out?"

A tipsy girl wearing nothing but a yellow bikini and wading boots rushed by between them, shrieking with laughter, pursued by a grinning guy in a sailing cap trimmed with gold braid. Greer sighed. These people were *so* not New Yorkers. She really ought to go back to the beach house before someone tried to hand her a fishing pole, or a live lobster, or some other Maine cliché in which she had no interest.

She took out a pale pink Chanel lip gloss and smoothed it onto her lips. "Come on, Hunter. We both know what that was all about upstairs." She kept her voice light, but she was serious.

Hunter's blue eyes darkened. "What makes you say that?"

Greer shrugged and gazed into the distance. She didn't need to explain it to him, did she? Did players really need to be reminded that they were players?

He put his hands on her shoulders and turned her toward him. "Whatever bad thing you're thinking about me right now — I'm not that kind of guy."

Greer refused to look into his eyes. She wanted to believe him, but she couldn't. It takes a player to know a player, and wasn't she one of the greatest players of them all? Her middle name might as well be Heartbreaker.

She reached up and gave him a peck on the cheek. "Thanks for a lovely evening," she whispered into his ear. "See you around."

And with that, she turned on her heel and waltzed away. And the part of her that wanted to turn back around and run to him? She pretended that part didn't even exist. She was Greer Hallsey, and she was Not Going To Be Played.

When the scruffy-looking band Chace had hired began playing a loud, atonal version of Alice Cooper's "School's Out," Jessica turned to Connor and pointed toward the steps that led down to the beach. "Let's get out of here," she yelled over the din. "These guys are even worse than the DJ."

Connor held up a finger, mouthed, "Wait," and dashed off through the crowd, leaving Jessica alone and slightly baffled. Where in the world was he running off to? She was about to get annoyed when he reappeared with a big grin on his face and a fresh beer in each hand.

She took the one he held out to her gratefully. "You think of everything," she said as they walked away from the noise.

He patted his chest in mock pride. "That's why they call me Connor Selden, Boy Genius." He paused and cleared his throat. "I mean, *Man* Genius."

Jessica giggled and slipped her arm around his waist. He lay his tan arm across her shoulders and gave her a squeeze.

They walked down the old wooden stairs, past the dunes, whose waving grasses made whispering sounds in the wind. A little ways off, they could see the lights of the pier glittering like tiny stars. When they got to the sand, they kicked off their shoes, feeling the cool grains between their toes.

The moon was almost full in the sky, and it created a line of white sparkles on the ocean. The breeze made Jessica shiver, and it blew her long, blonde hair into her eyes. Connor gently brushed it away.

"I missed you every single day," he whispered.

Jessica liked him so much she could hardly bear to look at him. "I missed you, too," she answered. She had spent so many nights lying in bed, thinking about being near him again. His short visit during the year had only made her miss him more once he left. She could hardly believe that they were finally together.

He put his finger under her chin and tilted her face up, and then he kissed her deeply. She held him tight against her and felt like she was melting into him. She wanted to kiss him forever — except, as she'd admitted to Greer and Lara, she wanted to do *more* than kiss him this summer. She wanted to go farther with him than she had with anyone, and she knew that Connor wanted the same.

They kissed until Jessica's knees felt weak, and then Connor pulled away. "Should we keep walking? Get a little farther away from the party?"

Jessica nodded. "Otherwise some drunk guys might show up and want us to play beer pong or something." Connor chuckled. They held hands as they walked along the edge of the ocean, the cool water lapping at their bare feet.

"I know where we can go," Connor assured her.

"You *should* know," she teased. "You're a local."

He laughed good-naturedly. "You have a point."

They walked quietly for a while. Jessica didn't feel the need to fill the silence — in fact, she relished it. It just proved that she and Connor felt so comfortable with each other that they didn't need to talk.

She breathed in the salty smell of the sea and the hint of sunscreen that lingered on her skin. *Ocean and Coppertone,* she thought. *Someone should make a perfume that smells just like it. They could call it Beach or Summer Sea or June, and they'd probably make a fortune.*

Up ahead, the sun-bleached trunks of a few old spruce trees had been gathered together to form a kind of shelter from the wind. Connor led her inside, and she saw little yellow wildflowers growing up out of the sand. The breeze seemed to hush itself, and the ocean's roar grew to fill its place.

"I like to come sit here sometimes," Connor confessed, sinking into the sand and patting the space beside him. "It's like my own little beach shack."

Jessica sat down beside him and put her head on his shoulder. "It's so nice and peaceful," she said. "Though, as you may have noticed, there's no roof, which means you can hardly call it a shack. It's pretty much just a bunch of logs." Connor poked her in the ribs and she laughed, protesting. "I'm not saying I don't like it! Look how beautiful everything around us is." She looked up at the moon above them, suspended like some kind of giant chandelier. "I think it's great."

Connor turned toward her. "I think *you're* great."

Jessica thought he might have blushed to hear himself say that, and because he was so sweet and she didn't want him to be embarrassed, she leaned forward and kissed him. He responded immediately, pulling her in close. Their tongues met and danced around each other, and their hands roamed up and down each other's bodies. After a while Jessica gently pushed Connor down so that he was lying in the sand. She bent over him, kissing him passionately, and then she let her hand wander down to his waistband.

Was now the time? she wondered. Were they finally going to do what they'd talked about? Sure, maybe it was a little soon — after all, they'd just been reunited — but she was ready.

As her fingers wandered across Connor's stomach she wondered if he was going to take off her shirt or if she should do it for him.

She felt his hands reaching for her. But instead of removing her clothing, they were motioning for her to stop. She sat up, confused.

Connor sat up, too, brushing a few grains of sand from his arms. "I don't think . . ." he began. "Maybe we should —" And then he stopped.

Jessica felt herself writhing in embarrassment. They'd talked about losing their virginity to each other for months, but now when she'd tried to move things forward, Connor had stopped her. She couldn't believe it.

Hurt and confusion bubbled up in her and she blinked away tears. Connor reached out and touched her cheek. "I just . . ." he said.

She waited for him to say more, but he didn't. And though she wanted to ask him what was going on, she couldn't form the words. Had she done something wrong? Had she somehow become a terrible kisser? All of a sudden she had a million questions, and she found that she couldn't ask a single one.

So she just stood up, hugging her arms around herself to hide her hurt, and walked out of the little hideaway. Connor got up and followed her toward home, but this time the silence between them wasn't as comfortable as it had been before.

"Two eggs, eyes open, pig on the side," Lara called to Earl, the portly cook, as she placed her ticket on the board in front of him.

"Got it," Earl grunted, flipping a pile of hash browns onto a plate.

It was a Friday morning at Ahoy Grill, and Lara was busy fetching coffee and breakfast for locals and summer people alike. She still sometimes giggled at the slang Earl encouraged her to use. "Two eggs, eyes open, pig on the side" meant two eggs, sunny-side up, with bacon. Chili was "a bowl of red" and "Adam and Eve on a raft" meant two poached eggs on toast.

She delivered two glasses of orange juice to a smiling, silver-haired couple and felt grateful to have her old waitressing job back. For one thing, she needed the money (the plane tickets to Ithaca and a new timing belt for her Beetle had put a serious dent in her savings account). And for another, she liked having something to do. Unlike Greer, Lara did not enjoy lying around in the sun all day, flipping through fashion magazines. And while Jessica was happy to do sporty things from dawn to dusk — surfing, biking, swinging lacrosse sticks with Connor, or whatever it was they did — Lara was not the athletic type, either. So having a job at one of Pebble Beach's most iconic restaurants suited her just fine.

She brushed her short bangs away from her forehead and quickly drank a glass of water. The only downside about working at Ahoy was that this summer she was doing it alone.

Last year, Drew had been waiting tables right beside her. They'd commiserated over the occasional bad tip or rude customer and shared laughs whenever Earl did his Evil Dick Cheney with a Shotgun impression. They'd taken their breaks together, eating lunch in the cramped back room while Earl muttered to himself over the grill and Richard, Ahoy Grill's manager, lounged in the corner, reading the Boston papers and cursing the bad luck of the Red Sox. All day long, as she worked, Drew had been there, a constant presence that always made her heart race and her skin flush. There was no getting around it: Ahoy Grill just wasn't the same without Drew.

She took an order for some doughnuts and coffee ("sinkers and suds" to Earl) and then leaned against the pink Formica counter to give her feet a little break. She'd forgotten how tiring waitressing could be, and though she'd worn sneakers — a pair of Chuck Taylor low tops — she wished she'd picked some with a little more arch support.

Lara sighed. Sometimes listening to her interior monologue was like listening to her grandma. Lara was seventeen years old! What was she doing moping about being lonely and complaining about her feet? Next thing she knew she'd be out on the shuffleboard court with the rest of the blue-haired old ladies moaning about the price of milk these days.

Richard sidled up beside her and slapped the *Boston Globe* on the counter. "The Sox!" he moaned. "That idiot Crisp charges the mound and he's out for seven games. I'm telling you, a bad temper will get you nowhere."

Lara, to whom this meant nothing — she'd never seen a baseball game in her life, not even on TV — just nodded and smiled. Which was fine; Richard could talk RBIs and shortstops and fastballs all day long, but he didn't really need anyone to pay attention to him.

She poured herself some coffee, even though she'd had four cups already and was practically shaking from the effects of the caffeine. Pretty soon she'd be so jacked up she'd be writing down orders in what looked like chicken scratches.

"Ramírez and Youkilis, too," Richard went on, glaring at the paper as if it had insulted him. "They practically killed each other last week, and they're on the same damn team!"

Lara pretended to listen, but her attention was suddenly drawn on the door, which had just opened to reveal a very, *very* cute guy. He was wearing a pair of worn-in jean shorts, a faded Bob Dylan T-shirt, and flip-flops. The sand that clung to his feet suggested he'd come straight from the beach. In one hand he held a battered and rather dirty doll, and with the other he was grasping the shoulder of a very pouty girl who looked about seven.

Lara hurried over to them. "Table for two?" she asked, offering him her warmest smile.

He had dark, glossy hair and deep brown eyes. He reminded Lara of Gael García Bernal in *Y tu mamá tam-bién*, a movie that she had seen at least five times because Gael was so incredibly cute.

The Gael look-alike nodded emphatically. "My sister here needs a bowl of something sweet before she throws another hissy fit." He rolled his eyes and smiled back.

Lara led them to a booth in the corner, feeling his eyes on the nape of her neck. Her cheeks began to flush. The immediate attraction she felt for this dark-haired boy surprised her, since she had just been thinking about how much she missed Drew.

But since Drew had taken himself out of the Pebble Beach picture by deciding to be a camp counselor for a bunch of snot-nosed third-graders somewhere in the Vermont woods, she was free to look, right?

Or maybe do more than look?

She put a little swing in her hips as she walked, and then felt silly.

Stop it, she chided herself. *He's just here for some ice cream. He's not here to order up a date with you.*

Brother and sister clambered into the booth, and the girl reached for her spoon and pointed it at Lara aggressively. "I want a banana split," she demanded.

Her brother snatched the spoon away. "Marcela," he warned, "if you can't be polite, you can't have any ice cream." He looked up apologetically at Lara. "She's been impossible today because our parents drove to the art museum without her." He paused and looked back at his sister. "Even though she said she didn't want to go," he added pointedly. "Even though she says art is stupid."

Marcela stuck her tongue out at him.

"So a banana split?" Lara asked, admiring the guy's patience, as well as his muscled, athletic body, which was so different from Drew's lanky leanness.

"Yes, please," he said, handing Marcela a stack of napkins in preparation for the inevitable mess.

Lara turned to the little girl. "You know what our cook calls a banana split? A *houseboat*! It's his special word for it."

Marcela raised her eyebrows, and her black eyes opened wider. "That's silly," she pronounced.

"I know!" Lara was encouraged by the girl's change in attitude. "So I'll bring you one houseboat right away." She turned to Marcela's brother. "What can I get for you?"

He glanced at the menu and then up at her. "Coffee, I guess. That's all for now."

"It's good here," she assured him. "I should know; I've already had about a gallon of it. My name is Lara. If you need anything else, just yell."

"Thanks," he replied. "I'm Marco."

Lara smiled at him. She always told customers her name, but they never offered theirs in return. Perhaps, she thought as she walked away, Marco was just a tiny bit interested in her, beyond her ability to bring him a cup of Ahoy Grill's strong, black coffee.

It was 11:15, the beginning of the lull between breakfast and lunch. Normally Lara would be occupying herself with prep work for the lunch rush, but she'd come in early that morning and gotten everything ready, which meant that now she was free to linger by Marco's table after she brought Marcela her banana split.

"My sailboat!" Marcela had squealed upon seeing the sundae, piled high with fresh whipped cream and topped with three glistening maraschino cherries.

Lara and Marco shared a smile, not bothering to correct her as she dove into the sugary treat.

"So are you in town for the summer?" Lara asked casually.

Marco nodded. "My dad grew up just south of here, and he likes to come back when he can. My mom loves it, too, even though she says the water's too cold. But she's from Chile — have you ever gone into the ocean in Chile? It's freezing. You ought to spell the country 'Chilly.' You know, like C-H-I-L —"

"I get it," Lara laughed. "Very funny."

"Oh, it's not funny at all; it's deadly serious," Marco said with mock sternness. "That ocean will freeze your Chuck Taylors off." He raised an eyebrow.

Involuntarily, Lara glanced down at her shoes, one of which had a big splotch of ketchup on it already. She wished she could waitress in cute sandals. How was she supposed to flirt wearing dirty sneakers, a red-checked apron, and a T-shirt that said, "Get Your Grill On at Ahoy"?

"Well, I'll be very careful the next time I'm in Chile," she answered, smiling and feeling a blush sting her cheeks.

Marco turned to his sister, who had a large dollop of whipped cream on her nose. "Hey, kiddo, you're supposed to eat that stuff, not inhale it. Snorting whipped cream is dangerous. It can be addictive, too. You don't want to end up on the streets, begging for a can of Reddi-wip, do you?"

Lara laughed. "Whipped cream is a gateway drug," she added. "Next thing you know you'll be shooting up Red Hots and Lemonheads, and let me tell you, that is not a path you want to go down."

Marco grinned. "Listen to Lara! She's seen it all, working here at Ahoy. Kids strung out on Pop-Tarts and root beer floats . . ."

Marcela, who was very happily eating her sundae, ignored them both. Lara wondered how long they could keep this joke up. Personally, she had a tendency to beat a joke into the ground, but she was trying to learn to quit when she was still ahead. Which was why, instead of talking about twelve-step programs for licorice addicts, she cleared her throat and asked Marco where his family was staying.

It turned out that their house was just half a mile from the Tuttles' trio of cabins.

"I've walked by your houses," Marco said, after Lara told him where the Tuttle family was staying. "They used to be beach shacks, and now they're more like Mies van der Rohe."

Lara raised her eyebrows. Mies van der Rohe? How many tall, to-die-for, cute guys had ever heard of the famous German architect, let alone could drop his name into casual conversation? Her interest in Marco ticked up a notch.

"They're pretty great," Lara allowed. "This is only my second summer in them. My mom married into the Tuttle family, and they've rented those houses forever. I mean, they rented the shacks, and then after those burned down and the new ones got built, they started renting them . . ." She felt herself babbling a little, and so she stopped and bit her lip.

"Lucky you," he said. "With all those people around, it must be like an endless party."

Lara thought of the big cookouts, the family picnics, and the nights she and Jessica and Greer had stayed up giggling until three in the morning. "Yeah, it sort of is."

Marco's dark eyes met hers. "Maybe you could invite me sometime," he said softly.

Lara felt her heart skip a beat. "S-sure," she stammered. Then she recovered herself and ran a hand through her hair. "I mean, if you think you can handle the crowd. I have cousins you can't win over with a single banana split, you know."

Marco took a sip of his coffee and then leaned back in the booth. "I think I can handle that," he said. "Why don't you give me your number?"

Before she could regret it — before she could think again of Drew — Lara scribbled her cell phone number on a blank ticket.

Marco took it with a smile and tucked it into his pocket. "I'll use this, you know," he warned.

The bell over the front door jangled, and Lara saw a party of five come tramping into the waiting area. The lunch rush was about to begin.

She started toward the hostess stand, and then turned back to Marco. "I dare you to," she said playfully, and then she walked away, feeling her spirits lift.

Operation Move On was under way.

7

The Pebble Beach Athletic Club was certainly no fancy New York health club, Greer mused as she slipped out of her eggplant-colored sheath in the no-frills locker room. CLAY, the gym Greer belonged to back in Manhattan, boasted cool, minimalist Zen decor and eucalyptus-and-mint-scented towels, not to mention a roof deck where one could get rubbed down, post-workout, by a very hot masseuse. The PBAC, on the other hand, reminded Greer of a high school gym. Its towels smelled like bleach, and there wasn't a masseuse in sight, unless that large, grumpy woman who'd checked her in was also certified in shiatsu.

Greer sighed as she shrugged on her tennis dress and

pulled her shiny, dark hair into a ponytail. She was so *not* the athletic type, but her mother had begged her to join her for a quick tennis game.

Normally Greer would have refused (and perhaps suggested her mother ask Jessica the Jock to play in her stead) but this summer she had two reasons for agreeing to this plan: (1) She was trying to be nicer to her mother, because she knew, deep down, that Cassandra was just trying to have a good vacation, and (2) She wanted to keep an eye on her mother, because she was pretty sure that Cassandra — in true, *Desperate Housewives* style — had been flirting with every pool boy, tennis coach, and golf pro in the greater Pebble Beach area.

Greer checked herself in the mirror, making sure her Ralph Lauren tennis dress clung to her in all the right places, and then dabbed a little sunscreen on her face before heading out to the court to meet her mother.

She saw her sitting on one of the benches by the courts, talking to another woman. By the stiff way her mother held her shoulders back and clutched at her racquet, Greer could tell she was *not* a fan of her bench companion. As Greer approached, she noticed that the other woman was about her mother's age and was similarly cosmetically enhanced: Greer could spot a boob job and a Botox addiction from a mile away.

"Oh, I just love Aspen," the woman was saying, waving her red talonlike nails through the air. "We stay in this absolutely wonderful inn —"

"Oh, Aspen, really?" Greer's mother said coolly. "I always preferred Gstaad myself."

The woman smiled a thin, disingenuous smile. "Well, I suppose if you're not at all concerned about the size of your carbon footprint, you could fly all the way to Switzerland," she responded.

Cassandra was unfazed. "Carbon footprint? Of course we care about our carbon footprint, Monica. That's why we charter a small, fuel-efficient jet." She fingered the diamond pendant she wore so that the three-carat stone flashed in the light. "And the Jacuzzis in our hotel are solar-heated, of *course.*"

Monica narrowed her eyes as she prepared her rejoinder. "Oh, you Jacuzzi? All that chlorine can really age the skin." She leaned in closer. "Have you moisturized recently?"

Greer suppressed a chuckle. When men tried to show each other up like this, she thought, it was called a pissing contest. But what was the term for two fortysomething women in short tennis skirts exchanging delicate barbs under the guise of polite conversation? Greer smiled to herself. *Two cougars flexing their claws*, she thought.

"Sorry to interrupt," she said sweetly, tapping her Tretorns on the pavement, "but don't we have a tennis game to play, Mom?"

Cassandra glanced up at her daughter and smiled. "Oh, darling, you weren't interrupting. You weren't interrupting anything at *all*."

Monica stood up, revealing a toned, tan body and plenty of diamonds of her own. "Yes, I think we were quite done," she huffed, and stalked off toward the locker room.

Greer poked her mother in the arm. "You don't have to be so awful, you know."

Cassandra laughed. "That provincial hausfrau thinks she's God's gift to the tennis pros. You should have seen her slobbering all over the manager. It was absolutely disgusting."

What Greer did not point out was that this was a pot-calling-the-kettle-black sort of situation, considering that her mother had been handing out her "business card" (Cassandra called herself an interior decorator, but the only homes she'd ever decorated were her own) to every male with a nice smile and a heartbeat.

"Well, Mom, maybe you can show her up in tennis," Greer suggested, leading her mother to their court.

Cassandra clapped her hands together gleefully. "That's exactly what I plan to do. Which is why I signed us up for lessons together, three times a week, until the end of summer, when we destroy that bleached blonde and her slutty daughter in the Pebble Beach Athletic Club Mother-Daughter Tennis Tournament."

Greer's mouth fell open. "Excuse me? Tennis lessons? I agreed to a *game*, Mom, a single, solitary game."

Cassandra pulled a visor down over her carefully coiffed hair. "Oh, please, Greer, what else do you have to do? You can't lie on the beach all the time."

"Oh, yes I can," Greer insisted. "Just watch me."

"I've already paid for the whole season," Cassandra went on. She turned back toward the clubhouse, adjusting her bracelets and then glancing at her watch. "The pro will be here any minute. In fact, I think I see him coming now."

Greer squinted in the bright sunlight, then remembered her Chanel shades and slid them down over her eyes. A tall, tanned figure wearing a PBAC polo loped toward them.

Wait.

It couldn't be — was it? She felt her stomach do a little flip.

Greer was glad that her sunglasses hid most of her face, because that meant they also hid most of her surprise. The instructor her mother had hired for them was none other than Hunter. As in, the extremely hot player Greer had made out with at the party.

"Mrs. Hallsey," Hunter declared, holding out his hand. "So wonderful to see you again."

Cassandra twittered and blushed, clearly awed by Hunter's charm. "This is my daughter, Greer," she informed him. "Greer, this is Hunter Brown."

Greer folded her arms across her chest and gazed stonily at them both through her shades. "We've met."

"Really?" Cassandra looked surprised. "Well, isn't that nice. You two are already friends."

Friends, Greer thought drily. *Is that what you call it when you jump each other five minutes after you've met?*

Hunter grinned at her, and Greer was struck again by how handsome he was. She could tell he saw right through her aloof act with those blue eyes of his. He was practically daring her not to smile back.

Then he turned to her mother. "I had the opportunity to make the acquaintance of your beautiful daughter at a party a week or two ago," he informed her, and Cassandra practically cooed with pleasure.

Greer stifled a snort. Yeah, he'd been able to "make her acquaintance." Was that what he called nibbling on her neck? But she had to hand it to Hunter: He sure knew how to charm the ladies.

"You didn't mention you worked here," she said, still not smiling at him.

Hunter shrugged. "There wasn't time, I guess." Then he winked. Really, he was ridiculously good-looking.

Greer sighed. She *so* wanted to be a good girl this summer, and Hunter was not going to make it easy, was he?

As they made their way onto the court for their first lesson, Hunter fell into step beside her. "See?" he whispered. "I'm the kind of guy you can bring home to your mother."

"All I need you to be now is the kind of guy who can improve my backhand," Greer hissed.

Hunter laughed. "Still a spitfire, I see. Well, listen, Ms. Heartbreaker, I *like* you, and I'm not going to let you slip away again."

Greer was trying to think of what to say when a beautiful, red-haired girl in a practically see-through beach cover-up passed by on the other side of the chain-link fence.

And Hunter, who had just been swearing his sincerest affection for Greer, stopped and stared.

I knew he was a player, Greer thought icily. Normally she liked being right about people, but she found little pleasure in it this time.

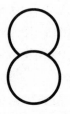

Jessica pulled the bedsheet up tightly over her body, and then, thirty seconds later, kicked it off again, flopping over onto her stomach and burying her face in her down pillow. After lying like that for a while, she realized that she was getting light-headed from lack of oxygen, and so she turned back onto her side.

Out the window she could see the moon dancing on the water. The reassuring sound of the surf filled the quiet room. But she was not reassured. She was awake and restless, thinking about Connor.

She sighed loudly and flopped over onto her other side.

"Good God," cried Lara from the bunk bed below her.

"What's your problem, Jess? It's like trying to sleep underneath a wrestling match or something."

From the double bed on the other side of the room (of course Greer had scored the double bed) came a snort of laughter. "It's true," Greer said, sounding sleepy herself. "You've been tossing and turning for an hour. What gives?"

Jessica stopped flopping around and lay still, staring up at the ceiling. She wasn't sure how to talk to her cousins about what was going on — or, rather, what *wasn't* going on — between her and Connor. Greer and Lara were so much more experienced with the physical stuff that Jessica felt embarrassed. She sighed again.

"Really, Jess," Lara said. "Enough sighing. Out with it."

"Fine," Jessica huffed, sitting up in bed and letting her legs dangle down over the edge. "It's about Connor."

"Duh," Lara cried, swatting at Jessica's feet. "It's not like we thought you were up there worrying about your lacrosse tryouts."

"Yeah," Greer added from the corner. "Though thank God you made varsity last year. You and Connor certainly practiced enough." She paused, then went on slyly. "Though I always thought you should have been kissing him the whole time rather than kicking his ass on the athletic field." She giggled, and Jessica tossed one of her pillows at her.

"This is serious, you guys," Jessica pleaded. She really needed their advice; otherwise she'd never sleep another moment in her life. She'd have to spend every night tossing and turning until Connor finally explained why he'd turned her down. She gathered her courage — it was so hard to talk about this stuff. "Remember how I told you that Connor and I had talked about . . . um . . . ."

"About losing your virginities together," Lara interjected helpfully.

Jessica nodded in the dark room, even though neither Lara nor Greer could see her. "Right. Well, I'm ready, and I thought he was, too. I mean, we talked about it, like, all year. But the other night, during the party, we were making out in this beautiful spot on the beach, and I thought we would, you know, go for it — or at least get *close* to it. But then he stopped me."

Greer whistled in disbelief. "A red-blooded American male actually discouraging a girl from going all the way? I've never heard of such a thing. Are you sure he's not some kind of alien, sent to study our strange human ways?"

Jessica heard Lara's bright laugh bubble up from the bed beneath her. "Yeah. There's obviously something deeply disturbed about a guy who doesn't want to do it with a hottie like you."

"Or maybe he's a cyborg," Greer offered thoughtfully, "or a robot like in that Bruce Willis movie."

Jessica knew her cousins were just trying to lighten the mood, but their teasing made her feel worse. She stared at the dark ceiling. "Seriously, guys, I don't get it. What do you think is going on? Do you think he doesn't like me as much as he used to? Or if it's not that, what's the problem? Maybe he . . ." She could barely make herself say the words. "Maybe there's . . . someone else."

She waited while her cousins thought for a moment.

"Obviously he adores you," Lara assured her from below, and Jessica felt instantly relieved. "Remember how he swept you up the moment he saw you? He wouldn't change his mind that fast. No boy is capable of such quick thinking."

Greer turned on her reading light and held up the copy of *Seventeen* magazine she'd been reading before they went to bed. She pointed to the cover. "It says in here that communication is the key to a great romance," she commented. "Personally I think a set of six-pack abs is more crucial, but I'm not the expert they chose to consult for this article. The point is, maybe you should ask Connor what's up."

Jessica fell back into her bed. "I can't," she wailed. "I'm too embarrassed!"

Lara got up from her bed and padded over to the window overlooking the rocky, moonlit beach. "Look," she said, pointing to the black outlines of the trees silhouetted against the sparkling water. "You're in one of the most romantic places on earth. But even romance demands practicality." She yawned and stretched sleepily. "So you need to plan a date night. A really, really great date night, where you dress up, you flirt, you share a little wine —"

"Then you seduce him!" Greer squealed.

Lara sighed. "Greer," she said, her voice sounding tired, "be serious. We're going for subtlety. Jessica tried throwing herself at him already and it didn't work. Connor needs *wooing*."

Greer folded her arms across her chest defiantly. "But I *was* being serious. You go on a great date — you know, eating dinner, watching the sun set, holding hands, all that — and then I guarantee you he'll be trying to take your clothes off by ten P.M."

Lara walked over and put her hand gently on Jessica's ankle. "You'll have to excuse Greer — she has the patience of a six-year-old."

Greer harrumphed from her corner and flipped the pages of her magazine.

"But she has a point," Lara went on, clambering back into her bunk. "If you don't feel like you can talk to Connor about this stuff right now, then don't. Instead you can just be sweet to him and enjoy a romantic evening together and see where things lead. But I promise you it's not about something you've done wrong, or some other girl he's suddenly decided that he likes."

Jessica let herself sigh one last time, and then she said, "Okay, you're probably right." She plumped up her pillow and pulled the jacquard comforter up to her chin. Her cousins were older and wiser, and she should trust them. "Thanks, guys. I think I feel a little better."

"Anytime," Lara said. "Now let's pester Greer about her love life."

At that, Greer dove down under the covers, prompting squeals from both Jessica and Lara.

"Tell, tell!" Jessica practically shrieked, immediately forgetting her woes. If cool-as-a-cucumber Greer was burying her head under the blankets, there must be a good reason for it. Or, more accurately, a hot-male reason for it.

After another few seconds, Greer reemerged with an embarrassed grin on her face. "Hunter Brown," she said mysteriously, and then pretended to be absorbed in her *Seventeen* magazine again.

"Stop torturing us," Lara cried, and Greer closed the magazine and looked up at them, blinking innocently.

"He's my tennis coach," Greer admitted after a moment, which sparked Lara to make a tsk-tsk sound. "Yeah," she went on, rolling her eyes, "I'm hot for teacher. But the thing is, it's not just that he's my coach." She gazed for a moment at the wall of Lara's movie posters and then went on. "It's that we already hooked up at Chace's party."

"Whoa, Speedy Gonzales! You met him that night and hooked up with him?" Jessica asked incredulously. She couldn't believe how fast her cousin moved. Were all New Yorkers as audacious as Greer?

"Arriba," Greer said drily, nodding as if it were no big deal. "Then I blew him off because he's got 'player' written all over him. I mean, he might as well have it tattooed on his forehead." A rueful smile appeared on her face and then quickly vanished. "He swears he's a good guy, but I don't buy it. He's really cute, and he's totally charming. But I saw him practically drool over some girl at the athletic club the other day. And he's telling me I can trust him?"

"Wow," Jessica said. She sympathized — she'd crushed out on a major player last summer (who also just happened to be Connor's older brother, Liam), and even though nothing had come of it, the memory still stung. She snuggled farther down into her bed and thought about how glad she was that she and Connor were together, even if things weren't particularly smooth between them at the moment.

From beneath her, Lara's soft voice came out with another suggestion. "What if you test Hunter's boyfriend potential, Greer?" she asked. "So you can find out if he means what he says, and see if his good-guy story holds up." Lara was full of clever ideas tonight, it seemed.

Greer looked doubtful in the soft glow of her reading lamp. "I swore off games, too," she said. "Even though I didn't write that down on our list of goals."

"Where is that list, by the way?" Jessica queried. "You'd better still have it."

Greer bristled slightly. "Of course I do. Your little secrets are safe with me."

Lara sighed and rolled over. "But back to the matter at hand, ladies. Greer, if you don't test Hunter, you might never know if he's angel or devil —"

Greer held up a manicured hand in surrender. "Fine, fine, you're right. I'll do it. I'll figure something out."

And Jessica, who always wanted to believe the best about people, added, "I'm sure you'll find out he's the perfect guy for you."

"Maybe," Greer said. But she sounded doubtful, and her expression was clouded.

Lara yawned loudly. "Okay, now that we've got everything settled, let's go to sleep. I've got to work tomorrow, unlike you lazy layabouts."

Greer and Jessica chuckled and then they all closed their eyes, though Jessica still tossed and turned a bit. This time, though, instead of worrying about Connor, she was planning the best date ever.

After nearly two weeks passed with no phone call from Marco, Lara began to regret giving him her number that day at Ahoy Grill. First her boyfriend (*ex-boyfriend*, the little voice in her head corrected her) had vanished into the Vermont woods, and then Marco had disappeared into the rocky coves of Pebble Beach. It was just one more blow to her ego. For all she knew, Marco had asked for her digits only so he could rope her into babysitting that crabby little sister of his. Lara was an only child — and glad of it — but somehow people always looked at her and thought "excellent babysitting material!" She couldn't for the life of her figure out why.

So when her phone rang on a Thursday at five with a number she didn't recognize, she almost ignored it. She was deep into Jane Austen's *Emma*, and was looking forward to a quiet night of reading and sipping iced tea on the patio. But then Greer walked by in some flowing beach-gown thing and said, "Please answer that. Your ringtone is really annoying."

So Lara had obeyed her, only to find Marco on the other end of the line. Her heart flipped over and before she could think, he was asking her if she wanted to go on a picnic.

Asking her out!

Lara hesitated for a few beats while Marco whistled non-chalantly into her ear. "Go ahead and put me on hold while you think about it," he teased. "I'll pretend I'm calling the credit card company or something. Those people take forever."

Lara laughed. What was the harm in a little picnic? "Sure," she said. "I'd love to."

Marco stopped whistling immediately. "Perfect. I'll grab the goods and then I'll be there in half an hour."

She almost told him yes, that sounded great, but then she realized that she didn't want to have to introduce him to any of the Tuttles — and especially not Jessica. Lara's desire for secrecy made her feel deceptive, which was a sentiment she did not enjoy. After all, she considered herself a gener-ally honest and trustworthy person. *And*, that annoying little voice in her head reminded her, *being sneaky is precisely the opposite of your summer goal.* "I want to stop keeping secrets from people I love," she'd said, and Greer had written it down in her terrible handwriting and then hidden the paper in her massive purse.

On the other end of the line, Marco cleared his throat. "Hello? Am I on hold again?"

Lara thought of his dark, laughing eyes, and his strong, tan shoulders. She remembered how he'd made her laugh that day at Ahoy with his silly pun about Chile. *Drew isn't your boyfriend anymore*, she reminded herself. *He chose camp over you.*

She took a deep breath. "How about I meet you at the pier?"

"Perfect," Marco said.

They agreed to find each other at the far end, near where the old men fished, and Marco assured her that she didn't need to bring anything but her pretty self. So Lara quickly slipped out of her tank top and cutoffs and put on a vintage sundress in a white and kelly green print, which she complemented with yellow flats and a big pair of white-framed sunglasses. She glanced at herself in the mirror as she nervously fluffed her short, black bob. She looked . . . what was the word? Gamine. A little Audrey Hepburn-ish, with a dash of flower child. The blue necklace Drew had given her for Christmas glittered in the hollow of her clavicle. (She liked it too much not to wear it just because she and its original purchaser were no longer speaking.)

She took one of the house bicycles and peddled slowly down the winding road to the pier, hoping the cool, salty breeze would ease the jitteriness she felt. As she passed by one of the picturesque white lighthouses that dotted the Maine coastline, she told herself that she wasn't necessarily going on a date. Because she didn't think she was quite ready for that yet. What she was ready for, though, was a big sandwich and a bag of chips, because it was nearly six o'clock and she was starving. Something about the ocean air made her ravenous.

Marco was leaning over the railing at the far end of the weathered pier, gazing down into the blue-green water. She went up to him and, striking up her courage, touched his shoulder warmly. He turned around, offering her a wide and welcoming smile.

"You look beautiful," he said, and she ducked her head in happy embarrassment. He pointed to the row of old men who lined up along the pier's edge, clutching fishing poles. "So I thought we could just grab one of the fish that these old dudes catch and fry him up down on the beach," he said. "What do you think?"

She stared at him. Was he being serious? She really didn't want to watch him gut some poor fish for her dinner.

But Marco reached out and laid his hand on her shoulder. "I'm kidding," he reassured her, still smiling. "I brought

Caprese sandwiches, deviled eggs, and a salad of mizuna greens and olives."

"Whew!" Lara breathed. "I was worried there for a minute." She loved the mozzarella, basil, and tomato of a *Caprese* sandwich, and though she wasn't sure what mizuna greens were, she was prepared to like them.

Marco turned and led her back along the pier the way she'd come, holding the picnic basket in one hand and wheeling her bike chivalrously with the other. She locked the old Schwinn to a rack near the parking lot, and then they navigated down along giant dark rocks until they found themselves on the pebbly beach.

"I considered getting takeout from Ahoy Grill," Marco admitted, "but then I decided you'd probably had your share of the blue plate special over there."

Lara nodded vigorously. "It's hardly even July and I'm already sick of the food there. I mean, it's good and all, but there's only so much of Earl's cooking a person can take. He puts six tablespoons of butter into *everything*."

"I feel that way about my dad's cooking," Marco said, carefully sidestepping a jellyfish that had washed onto the shore. "He thinks he's a gourmet chef or something, just because he sprinkles freshly chopped herbs over things. I keep telling him that Hamburger Helper is Hamburger Helper no matter how much rosemary you add to it."

Lara laughed knowingly — she could sympathize. "My mom's not the greatest cook, either. She's kind of a get-it-from-the-freezer-section-at-Trader-Joe's-and-pop-it-in-the-oven person." Her mother had gotten more interested in cooking since her marriage to Mike, who was himself quite skilled in the kitchen, but she still tended to cook out of boxes and cans more than she ought to. Lara and Mike had been trying to educate her, though; they'd finally convinced her that making her own tomato sauce for pasta was almost as easy as — and infinitely better than — sauce from a jar.

Marco's dark eyes flashed with humor. "Well, it's a good thing we didn't have to rely on either of them for our picnic. Here, does this look like a nice spot?"

They'd come to a little cove where the water lapped gently at the shore. Little sandpipers dashed this way and that along the edge of the water, and above them the gulls wheeled and turned in the sky. Slender, white boats with multicolored sails sliced across the bay.

"It's perfect," Lara said, and she meant it. She sank down onto a large rock that was still warm from the sun. This was nothing like the summers she'd spent in Chicago, sweltering in the humidity and bored out of her mind. Here the air was clean and fresh and she felt truly, magically alive.

Marco spread out a soft, blue blanket and she abandoned her rock to sit cross-legged on it while he laid out their spread. Besides the food he'd told her about, there were also sliced fresh strawberries with mint, two bars of dark chocolate (her favorite), and a bottle of *vinho verde*.

"*Vinho verde* — green wine?" Lara asked, reading the label.

Marco nodded. "It's Portuguese. It's a young wine, with a little bit of fizz. Very refreshing." He paused. "Not to sound like some snooty wine guy or something. I like a good India Pale Ale myself, but I thought you looked like a wine drinker."

"Very perceptive," Lara acknowledged. "So are you going to pour me some already?"

Marco grinned and obeyed, and they clinked their plastic cups together. "Here's to an excellent summer," Marco said.

"Cheers," Lara added, and they both took a sip.

As they ate, they complained about high school and shared war stories about bad after-school jobs. Lara was surprised to find that they had a lot in common: They shared a love for film noir, the novels of Graham Greene, and pizza with anchovies. They both hated extreme sports, the starchy sauces on Chinese food, and the band Fall Out Boy.

"Pete Wentz?" Lara asked. "Count me out!"

Marco shook his head vigorously. "He's almost as bad as Ashlee Simpson-Wentz."

The food Marco had packed was delicious, and the wine was sparkly and tart and delectable — like drinking champagne mixed with apple cider. Lara found herself draining her glass more quickly than she was used to, and pretty soon she felt pleasantly loopy.

She lay back on the blanket and stared at the slowly darkening sky. "There are so many stars here. In Chicago I can only see about ten, and that's only if there's no moon. What about you? What's Albany like?"

Marco grimaced slightly; apparently his hometown was not one of his favorite places. "We're only there because my mom is head of Latin American studies at the university. She's hoping for a job at Bowdoin, or maybe Bates or Colby, so we can be back in Maine." He popped the last deviled egg in his mouth. "We're *all* hoping she gets one. We miss it here. We used to live here year-round, back when Marcela was a baby."

Lara imagined a young Marco running up and down the beach chasing birds and hunting for seashells. The thought made her smile.

"What are you thinking about?" Marco asked softly.

Lara hesitated, and then answered honestly. "You," she said.

Marco raised his eyebrows slightly, and he seemed

about to make a joke. But then he must have thought better of it, because he leaned toward her.

He's going to kiss me, Lara thought. *What should I do?* But before she could answer her own question, his lips were against hers. They were soft and warm and gentle, and she felt herself responding, almost against her will. An image of Drew flashed in her mind, but she closed her eyes more tightly until it vanished. As she opened her mouth and their tongues touched, she felt a surge, like an electric current, travel from her lips down through her body and all the way to her toes. She let herself fall into the kiss, and then after a few moments she reluctantly pulled away.

"Um," she said.

Marco looked at her with his beautiful dark eyes. "Too fast?" he asked. "Should I have waited until after dessert to kiss you?"

Lara laughed shyly. "I just . . . Oh, I don't know." She didn't want to tell him about her recent heartbreak, but the words were at the tip of her tongue.

Marco shrugged good-naturedly. "All right," he said. "Let's back up a bit. We were talking about Maine. And before that you were saying how you don't approve of digital cameras because you feel that the impermanence of the digital image only contributes to the throwaway consumerist culture that we live in."

Lara laughed and felt her cheeks turn red. "God, do I really sound like that?"

"*And*," Marco went on, even though she held up her hands in protest, "you were also talking about how our consumerist system, which equates conspicuous consumption with personal well-being, economic progress, and social fulfillment, is a recipe for social and ecological disaster."

Lara put her hands over her ears. "Stop!" she cried. "Please stop." It wasn't that she didn't believe in the truth of what she'd said — it was just that it sounded so . . . well, *pretentious* coming out of Marco's mouth. "I blame my diatribe on your *vinho verde*," she announced, folding her arms in defiance. But it was cute how much attention he'd paid to what she said.

"Oh, yeah," Marco said. "*Vinho verde* often induces anti-capitalist fervor. It says so on the back of the bottle." He pointed to the label.

She swatted his broad shoulder. "Shut up," she giggled.

"All kidding aside, though," he offered, "I do think you have a point. We waste way too much here in America."

Lara sighed. It was true. But she didn't want to talk about serious stuff anymore. She wanted to eat her dessert and then kiss Marco again. She glanced over at him, and found that he was gazing at her intently. By the look in his eyes, she could tell that he didn't care one bit about the dark chocolate he'd brought, or the fresh strawberries.

She smiled at him shyly, and then leaned a little toward him. And then Marco reached out and cupped her face with his hands. She slid her arms around his waist. After another minute, they were kissing again, hungrily. She felt his hands moving over her dress. She let out a little moan that was part pleasure, part protest. She felt like she shouldn't be doing this — wasn't a person supposed to wait a little while before hooking up with someone new? — but it felt so good. She shifted around to get more comfortable in the sand and Marco leaned over, pressing his body against hers.

Her fingers traced a line up his smooth back and then reached down to grasp his hips, pulling them against hers. She heard Marco's breath in her ear.

But even with her arms around Marco, Lara still couldn't quite shake the thought of Drew. *Who said anything about the rest of our lives?* he'd asked her. *No one did*, she thought fiercely.

Then Marco buried his face in her neck and kissed her collarbone and nibbled on her ear, and after that she thought only of him.

They lay like that for an hour, just kissing and touching each other, though to Lara it felt like only a few minutes. Then Marco reluctantly pulled himself away from her. "I promised my folks I'd be home at eleven," he said. "We're heading out for a really early sail."

Lara sat up and rearranged her dress, which had gotten very wrinkled in their make-out session. "It's probably for the best," she allowed. "This isn't the most private place in the world."

"I know," Marco said. "Those seagulls were totally checking us out. They're so jealous."

Lara tossed her napkin at him, shaking her head, but Marco just grinned.

After they kissed good-bye — for another half an hour — Lara biked home through the beautiful Maine night, feeling giddy, pleased, and only slightly tipsy.

She found Greer lounging on the deck with a glass of Uncle Carr's scotch and a copy of *Vanity Fair*. She raised her eyebrows when Lara appeared and looked her up and down. "What were *you* doing?" she asked, a hint of a smile playing on her lips.

Lara glanced around to make sure that they were alone. "I was out with the greatest guy," she whispered. "It wasn't supposed to be a date, but I think it turned into one."

Greer's eyes widened. *"Tell,"* she hissed.

"His name is Marco and he's half Chilean and he is probably the best kisser that the world has ever known,"

Lara gushed. Then she stopped herself. "It's terrible, I know. I mean, Drew and I are barely broken up. I mean, we are, but we never talked about it. We just — we just stopped talking to each other."

"And now he's snoring inside a tick-infested sleeping bag somewhere in Vermont." Greer reached out a reassuring hand. "Don't worry your pretty little head about it," she counseled. "You just do what makes *you* happy."

That seemed a little selfish to Lara. But then she thought back to the picnic and laughing with Marco. He had definitely made her happy — why should there be a problem with that?

She looked earnestly at her cousin. "You can't tell Jessica, though. This is a secret."

Greer smirked. "As the guardian of our Classified List of Summer Goals, let me remind you that I am excellent at keeping secrets. I had a bichon frise puppy for an entire year before my mother discovered him, you know. I can certainly keep my mouth shut about your Marco."

Lara lay back on the lounge chair next to Greer and took a sip of her cousin's scotch. "Phew," she spluttered. "That's strong."

"Wuss," Greer giggled. "But seriously. Your secret is safe with me."

Lara sighed. It was unfortunate to have such a big secret. But she let herself be reassured by Greer's reasoning. She could get to know Marco a lot better in the coming weeks, and Jessica never had to be the wiser. "Okay, Greer, you're right," she said firmly. "Ignorance is bliss."

"Amen to that," Greer agreed, and snatched her scotch back.

"Are you sure this looks okay?" Jessica queried as she modeled one of Greer's tube miniskirts for her cousins. She was showing way more leg than she was used to revealing, and the cute little lacy top she'd borrowed from Lara was definitely formfitting. She looked down at her chest. Had it always been that big?

"You look amazing," Lara reassured her. "No one would take you for a jock at all. You look more like a blonde Jessica Biel or something. Hot."

"Heidi Klum," Greer called absently. She was busy putting her own outfit together for some mystery date, Jessica guessed. After all, it was hardly like Greer to spend a Friday night in the house, parked in front of a plasma TV screen.

"So you've got the whole Operation Seduce Connor Selden planned?" Lara asked, reaching out to adjust the strap of Jessica's bra, which had slipped down her arm.

Jessica nodded excitedly. "Dinner in town, then dessert by Knight's Pond, where the water is conveniently warm enough . . ."

"For skinny-dipping!" Lara squealed.

Jessica blushed and then smiled. "Just in case he needed some encouragement to take his clothes off," she admitted.

"Brilliant," Greer remarked approvingly. Her voice was muffled, since she was halfway into a black Zac Posen. Then her head reappeared and she shook her brown hair and stuck her arms into the little cap sleeves. "Planned like a true fox. Whoever said little Jessi couldn't be crafty?"

"Jess*ica*," Lara and Jessica said at the same time, and then they all laughed.

"But get out of here; you're going to be late!" Greer warned. She tossed Jessica the keys to her Lexus. "I know you'll take excellent care of Sadie, so I won't even bother warning you that if you dent her or scratch her, I will break both of your legs."

Jessica giggled and thanked her cousins, then gave herself one last look in the mirror. She did look good; her blonde hair — already lighter from the sun — hung in loose waves around her shoulders, and her green eyes, highlighted with a silvery shadow, glowed above her tan cheeks.

"Bye!" she called, and dashed out the door.

Less than twenty minutes later, she and Connor were sitting at a corner table near the window at Chez Suzette, a sweet little French café with a view of the harbor. Connor had on his best white shirt and had actually gone so far as to tuck it into his khaki pants. He looked cute and clean and vaguely nervous, like a guy at a job interview or the first day of college or something.

Connor poured some sparkling water into both of their glasses and then looked around him at the pale blue walls and the roses on all the tables.

"So in a way, this is our first real date," he said. "I mean, we can't count all those lacrosse practices last summer or anything."

Jessica nodded. "I thought it was about time we saw each other in something besides swimsuits and athletic gear." She paused, hoping he would compliment her outfit, and when he didn't, she kicked him lightly in the shin.

He jumped. "Sorry — I mean, of course, you're right. And you look amazing."

Jessica grinned. Connor's compliment was obviously sincere, even if he'd had to be reminded to make it. "Thanks."

When the waitress brought them their food — lobster bisque and sole meunière for Jessica, steak frites and an endive and frisee salad for Connor — they looked at each other and snickered. It was so fancy, with gold linen napkins and the multiple sets of forks! Jessica hardly knew which one to choose, and from the look of it, Connor was no more experienced with complicated place settings than she was. But the food was delicious, and they were both starving because they'd been in the ocean all day.

As they ate, Jessica played a little footsie with her date, just to make sure he didn't forget about her while he was devouring his steak. And she did her best to keep the conversation away from sports, Xbox games, or anything else really low on the romance spectrum.

"I know I'm going to be stuffed in a minute," Connor said, interrupting her story about Greer's crush on Hunter Brown. "But I still want dessert."

Jessica shook her head firmly. "Can't have it here," she told him.

"Why not?" Connor looked so baffled and disappointed that she laughed out loud.

"I have a different plan for us." She gave him a significant — and what she hoped was sexy — look.

He whistled. "You sure know how to show a guy a good time."

"Just you wait," Jessica said in her best attempt at a sultry, seductive voice. (*It wasn't half bad, either!* she thought.)

Connor's eyebrows very nearly disappeared under his bangs. "Wow," he said. "There's something different about you tonight."

Jessica grinned at him but said nothing. So far, things were going exactly as she planned.

There was a slight chill in the air as Connor and Jessica walked along the forested path to Knight's Pond. Jessica led the way, carrying (despite Connor's attempts to be chivalrous) a canvas bag and a little cooler that contained their dessert — two slices of Aunt Trudy's to-die-for lemon cake with a container of raspberry coulis and a tub of fresh whipped cream to top it off.

When they came to the little sandy beach at the edge of the water, Jessica unfolded a blanket and motioned for Connor to sit down.

"Isn't this nice?" she said. "It's so private and quiet. I love the ocean, but sometimes I think I might love lakes and ponds better."

Connor nodded as he tried to peek into the cooler. Clearly he'd already digested the steak and was in need of another massive calorie infusion. "This is where I learned to swim, you know," he told her. "My mom taught me and my brother in this very pond."

"Leave the dessert alone!" Jessica laughed. "Let's just sit here for a minute. I, at least, need to let my dinner digest."

Connor watched with interest as she brought out the three beeswax candles she'd swiped from the dining room and lit them. The gentle breeze made the flames feint and sputter, but they gave everything around them a warm, golden glow.

"Nice," he said softly, and she smiled at him. Then she brought out the cake and dished it out onto their two plates, surrounding the golden slices with the raspberry sauce and dabbing whipped cream on top.

She sighed happily. It was so beautiful here. Above them, the leaves of an oak tree whispered and she could hear the birds singing good night to one another. Soon the bats would come out (unlike Greer, Jessica wasn't afraid of them at all) and perform their evening acrobatics in the air.

It was shaping up to be the perfect night. Pretty soon, Jessica knew, she and Connor would kiss. And if things went as planned, tomorrow she wouldn't be a virgin anymore. The thought made her nervous, but not so nervous as to change her mind.

She unbuttoned the top button of her blouse to reveal

the lacy edge of her bra, and then she reached out and touched Connor's leg.

"Remember last year, how you lost that bet to me and you had to go skinny-dipping in front of everyone?"

"How could I forget it," Connor moaned. "My brother teased me about that for weeks."

"How about you get me back?" Jessica offered. "What if we make some bet right now and if I lose, I'll go skinny-dipping?"

"I like the sound of that," Connor acknowledged. "I bet you can't eat that cake you brought us in four bites."

"You're on," Jessica said. Even though she wanted to enjoy the cake slowly, she took three big bites to make it look like she was trying. And then there was one mound of it left on her plate, and she forked it up. Even though she could have fit it all in her mouth, she didn't. She pretended she couldn't, and then she made a morose face.

"I lose," she said, though secretly she wasn't sad at all.

Connor clapped his hands delightedly. "Skinny-dip! Skinny-dip! Now you can bare your white butt in front of everyone we know."

Jessica stood up. "That's not exactly what I had in mind," she said softly. Then, before she could lose her nerve, she unbuttoned her blouse and her bra, letting both of them fall to the ground. Connor's eyes widened as she stepped out of her skirt. She was overcome by shyness then, even though it was dark out. Because she didn't want to fail in her seduction objective, she began to walk quickly toward the water, and at the edge she slipped off her panties and then plunged into the cool pond.

The water closed over her head and filled her ears. She kicked her arms and legs and then came up to the surface, wiping the water from her eyes. "The temperature is perfect!" she called. "Why don't you come in?"

Connor hesitated for a moment.

"What," she teased, "are you chicken or something? I dare you to come get me."

Connor would never back down from a dare; she knew that much. And indeed, he stood up, stripped quickly, and came dashing toward her into the water. "Not chicken!" he cried, splashing toward her.

She reached for him and pulled him close, and the next thing she knew they were kissing passionately. She loved the feel of his skin against hers, warm and smooth in the cool water. She let her hands wander down his arms and toward his stomach. She heard him inhale as her hands went farther south.

"Jessica," he whispered.

"Mmm," she said, kissing him more. Over his shoulder, the moon danced in the water.

He pulled away from her and took her face gently in his hands. He gazed intently into her eyes. "Look," he said, "I know this is what we talked about. But I think we should cool it a little."

Jessica's stomach fell with a *thud,* and she treaded water to move away from him. Suddenly, she was freezing in the cool night air. She couldn't believe what she was hearing. He was stopping her *again?* Connor tried to lean in to kiss her, but she wanted no part of it. She quickly turned around and splashed her way to the sandy shore.

Fuming and hurt, she snatched up a towel from the canvas bag and put on her clothes, as quickly as possible. Her cheeks burned with humiliation. Why did he keep preventing her from going any further? Hadn't they agreed to be each other's firsts? Maybe he needed some kind of engraved invitation, she thought bitterly. She remembered Greer asking what kind of normal American male would try to stop a girl from having sex. *I'd certainly like to know the answer to that,* Jessica thought. She wondered if the problem was him or her. Was she doing something wrong, or was he?

"Jessica, wait," Connor called.

But she was already packing up her things. He could make his way home by himself, she decided. She wasn't going to spend another minute with a person who kept rejecting her.

As she stomped down the path toward Greer's car, she heard Connor's voice, faint but insistent. "Hey," the disembodied voice said. "Jessica, please come back . . ."

But she kept on walking. His rejection stung too much, and she needed to be alone to recover her dignity.

She climbed into Greer's convertible, and as she drove down the winding road beneath the silvery moon, tears pricking at the corners of her eyes, her phone beeped with a text.

She slowed to a crawl along the deserted lane so she could read the message. It was from Connor. I'M SORRY, it said. I LOVE YOU.

Even though she was still hurt and angry, her heart swelled when she read that. She pulled over to the side of the road, clutching the phone in her hand, as conflicting thoughts raced through her mind. Should she keep driving? Or should she go back to him? She felt torn between desire and pride. He *loved* her! On the other hand, she couldn't understand why, if he really did, he always pushed her away.

Sadie's engine rumbled quietly as Jessica sat still, gripping the leather-wrapped wheel. She needed time to think, time to process Connor's inexplicable behavior. Feeling suddenly exhausted, she rested her forehead against the steering wheel, and as she did so she seemed to hear her mother's voice. *Sleep on it, darling*, Clare Tuttle always said whenever Jessica was upset. *Things are always clearer in the morning.*

She sat up and gazed into the star-studded July sky.

There was a strange fluttering feeling in her stomach. What was happening? Things were so weird with Connor, but she had the evidence of his love for her in her hand. And love meant everything, didn't it? As she sat in Greer's fancy convertible on the side of the empty road, she realized that — despite the tension and confusion he was causing her — she loved him, too.

And that's what matters, she whispered. *Everything else will work out just fine.*

Before she pulled back onto the road to drive the rest of the way home, Jessica sent Connor a text. LOVE U 2, she wrote. WE'LL FIGURE THIS OUT.

She hoped he knew what "this" meant. Because she didn't think she could take another round of rejection.

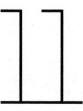

The Fourth of July passed uneventfully for the Tuttles this year, and the family's traditional break from barbecuing left Greer with lots of time to sit on the beach and think about Hunter Brown.

Gazing at the ocean from her lounge chair was certainly beautiful, but it hadn't yet given Greer the clarity she was looking for. Though Hunter claimed innocence and decency in all facets of his life, Greer remained unconvinced of his trustworthiness. After all, she'd thought Brady was the perfect guy, and look how *that* had turned out. (She was still sort of wishing for a giant storm that would render him green with seasickness and throw what's-her-face overboard.)

Of course, that hadn't prevented her from starting to

spend a lot of time with Hunter. After their first tennis lesson, he'd talked her into getting a drink in the clubhouse, and her resistance to his charms had only gotten weaker ever since. And she had to admit, his affectionate text messages and the walks along the beach they'd taken had been sweet.

But Greer had never met a guy as cute as Hunter who didn't come with big problems. The cutest guys were either (a) big-time players, (b) gay, or (c) some kind of handsome sociopath. Like that gorgeous ski instructor she'd met in the Swiss Alps, who turned out to be a pathological liar and occasional klepto who had a trunk full of ugly tourist souvenirs he'd stolen from various gift shops. Thank goodness she'd found that out before she lost her head and hooked up with him.

But it remained to be seen *exactly* what was wrong with Hunter. And to figure it out, Greer Hallsey was a girl with a plan.

Step 1: Enlist Lara's help (Jessica was too innocent for games such as these). Step 2: Place Hunter in enticing situation. Step 3: Confirm him as either (a) player, (b) gay, or (c) sociopath.

Greer was pretty sure that (b) wasn't an issue, considering the eagerness with which he'd kissed her. But he could still be (c) and she was willing to bet Sadie the Lexus on (a).

Lara had been reluctant to assist Greer at first, claiming she didn't like schemes. But Greer had bribed her by promising her the vintage Christian Lacroix dress that Greer had bought for a song (well, $600) at INA in SoHo.

Unable to resist a seventies gown as glamorous as that one, Lara had agreed, and now she was wearing Greer's most see-through shirt and a micromini, complemented by enough makeup to walk the line between runway fashionable and downright slutty.

Greer, who was hiding behind an azalea bush near the Pebble Beach Athletic Club tennis courts, shoved her cousin forward. "There he is," she whispered. "He's in the green shirt. Now, go over there and tell him you want tennis lessons. *Private* tennis lessons. As in maybe he wants to come teach you in your bedroom or something."

Lara turned back and rolled her eyes at Greer. "Please! That is *ridiculous*. But I'll come up with something, trust me." She started to walk away, swinging her hips suggestively. Then she turned around for one final glance at Greer. "By the way," she added, "this is so horribly embarrassing that I'm going to need you to give me your little 1950s clutch for this, too."

"Whatever!" Greer exclaimed. "Just go!"

She watched surreptitiously as Lara pranced over to Hunter, who looked up at her with obvious interest. Greer couldn't hear what Lara was saying, but by the way Hunter seemed to be staring at her, she was pretty sure that it was highly suggestive.

Every time Hunter opened his mouth, Lara threw back her head and laughed as if he were the most brilliant wit she'd ever encountered. She touched his arm, too, and twirled her short hair around her fingers the way girls do when they like a boy. Greer was impressed; she hadn't pegged Lara for a Class A flirt, but it turned out she was extremely good at it.

Lara bent down to scratch her ankle, ostentatiously showing Hunter her tan legs (tan thanks to nearly a whole bottle of Estée Lauder self-tanner, Greer thought wryly). *Damn, she's good!*

Their conversation went on so long that Greer began to wonder if Lara had forgotten her assignment and was hitting on Hunter because she wanted him for herself. But after a few more minutes, Lara came waltzing back to the azalea bush with a satisfied smirk on her face. And Hunter watched her the whole way, looking highly interested.

The girls snuck around to the side of the clubhouse, where Greer quizzed Lara on Hunter's behavior.

"You could just drown in his eyes," Lara said dreamily, and Greer punched her (but not too hard).

"Hello!" she cried. "You're supposed to be scoping him out for me, not for your own self!"

Lara laughed. "I'm just kidding. You know I like Marco. I mean, Drew. Oh, God, I mean —"

"Oh, whatever!" Greer interrupted. "He was hitting on you, wasn't he?"

"Well," Lara began.

"I most certainly was not," said a voice, and Greer whirled around to see Hunter standing behind her, looking distinctly unamused.

"Uh-oh," Lara whispered, her face going pale beneath the bronzer Greer had slathered on.

Greer's first instinct was to run and hide in the azalea bush again. But that was hardly her style. She tossed her hair defiantly: Greer Hallsey would run from no man! Though she could feel the mortification building in each and every pore, she drew herself up to her full five feet nine inches.

"I saw the way you looked at her," she accused. "You looked like some jackal eyeing his prey."

"Interesting metaphor," Hunter responded coolly.

"Um, I think I should get going," Lara whispered, and then turned and fled as quickly as she could in the come-hither heels that Greer had made her wear. "Also, by the way, that's a simile," she called over her shoulder.

"Do you deny it?" Greer asked haughtily.

Hunter swung his tennis racquet casually at his side. "I

was looking at her pretty closely; I'll admit that. But it was only because I was trying to figure out where I'd seen her before." He paused. "I'd just about put my finger on it when I saw your head peep out of the bush over there. Then I remembered that I saw you two walk into Chace's party together. Really, Greer, is that the level you want to stoop to?"

Greer resented his holier-than-thou tone. Who did he think he was, talking to her like he was her high school principal? "I'm just calling it like I see it. You're a player, and there's no getting around it, so you might as well admit it."

Hunter bristled and his blue eyes grew cold. "May I remind you that you're the one who made the first move at Chace's party? And you're the one who ran off afterward, even though I tried to make you stay? It's like you were so sure I was going to blow you off that you felt the need to blow me off first."

Though he had a point, Greer would be damned if she was going to admit it. "Maybe if the conversation would have been more scintillating, I would have stayed," she quipped. Over Hunter's shoulder, she saw Lara climb onto a bike and ride away. It occurred to her, much too late, obviously, that it would have been smart to enlist a girl who wasn't her cousin in the Hunter Trap.

"You weren't very interested in talking, as I recall," Hunter answered.

Damn, Greer thought. *He's got another point.* Since — for once in her life — she was unprepared with a snappy rejoinder, she simply gazed at him coolly. Usually guys crumbled in the face of her hazel-eyed stare.

But Hunter held his ground. "I'll admit, I like to look at a pretty girl. Find me a guy who doesn't. But you ought to be more understanding, Greer. From what I've heard you're not that innocent yourself. I mean, seducing me at Chace's wasn't exactly a first-time thing for you, was it?"

Whoa, Greer thought. *Is he calling me slutty? This is so not the direction I want the conversation to go.* Her past was past for a reason. "That's none of your business," she snapped.

Hunter glared at her. "You know what? I don't need this hassle. I like you, Greer, but I'm not going to put up with your crap. I don't do mind games." Then he turned on his heel and stormed off.

Greer was left alone in the shadow of the Pebble Beach Athletic Club locker room. After standing there for a moment, still fuming, she pulled her sunglasses back down over her eyes and stalked off in the other direction. She was furious, yes, but deep down in the pit of her stomach, she was also very sad.

Seagulls fluttered through the blue July sky as Lara and Marco sailed around the bay, one sailboat among dozens plying the calm waters. Clouds so white they seemed to glow passed by overhead, occasionally offering a moment of shade. Lara set down the zinc oxide she'd been reapplying to her still-ivory skin and picked up the operation manual she'd discovered underneath her seat cushion.

"Scupper, luffing, spar, jib — what do these words mean?" Lara asked, pointing to the book's baffling pages. "It's like a foreign language."

"A scupper is a drain in the cockpit," Marco said patiently as he expertly piloted them out of the mouth of the bay toward a small rocky island. "And luffing is what happens when a sail's not secured correctly or when you head too far into the wind, and —"

"Oh, blah blah blah," Lara interrupted playfully, leaning back against the cushions and enjoying the feel of the sun and the wind on her face. "I don't really care, you know. Just like you don't care that Earl calls corned beef on toast 'shit on a shingle.'"

Marco laughed. "Touché!" He cranked the wheel to the left and the boat curved south to skirt the island, which, Lara could now see, was inhabited by a vast number of fluttering dark birds. They'd been sailing for three hours already, and it was almost time for Marco to pick up Marcela from her arts camp. ("If she brings me another potholder or God's eye," Marco had muttered, "I don't know *what* I'm going to do.")

Lara had learned a little bit about sailing — Marco had let her steer for a while — but mostly she'd just enjoyed learning more about Marco. She discovered that he, too, had a soft spot for The Feelies and early R.E.M, and that he preferred independent films to studio blockbusters any day. He even knew a little bit about art (he loved Francis Bacon and Andy Warhol in particular), which she found very sexy. Drew had only listened to the latest music and had had little patience for museums.

In short, Marco was an ideal new guy for her. And

needless to say, she still hadn't mentioned anything to Marco about his immediate predecessor. Why rock the proverbial boat, when they were sailing along so smoothly?

It seemed only moments passed before Marco was bringing them back into the harbor and guiding them into the boat's berth. Lara sighed. She wished that their date — she could call it that now, couldn't she? — didn't have to end. She could have spent the whole day floating around Penobscot Bay, watching the seagulls swoop and dive above her and listening to Marco tell her stories about backpacking in the mountains of Chile. And he, in turn, had obviously enjoyed her tales of the freaky inhabitants of her Chicago neighborhood, like the one about how her neighbor, a man who insisted on being called Mr. Bojangles, had once dressed up in a grass skirt and performed a hula dance on his fire escape. (To this day, nobody knew why.)

Lara stepped reluctantly onto the dock and briefly struggled for balance.

Marco laughed. "It takes a little while to get your land legs back," he warned her. "Don't fall into the water or anything."

"If I do," she asked flirtatiously, "will you jump in and save me?"

"Of course," he replied gallantly. "I would never let a beautiful woman drown."

Lara smiled to herself: He had called her beautiful!

He leaned in to kiss her good-bye, and she reached up to hug him tightly. "See you again soon, I hope?" he whispered, and she nodded. She *definitely* wanted to see him again soon.

The blissful glow she felt biking home from the harbor survived a near sideswipe by a woman in a convertible (Lara gave her the finger, of course) and the struggle to lock her bicycle to the half-dozen others parked by the side of the Tuttle beach house (the other bikes kept falling over onto her toes). Then she walked onto the big porch and felt her cheer get slammed away by a giant wave of shock.

There on the porch was a huge bouquet of yellow roses bearing a card with her name on it — and none other than Drew Tuttle peering out from behind them. Lara stumbled, and very nearly fell off the deck in surprise.

Drew rose, smiling. But Lara just stood there as guilt and nervousness — and yes, even a bit of happiness — roiled around in her gut like some kind of complicated emotional soup.

"I can't . . . I can't believe . . . What are you *doing* here?" she spluttered.

He walked toward her and folded her into a hug. "I missed you," he said into her hair. "I missed you so much." He squeezed her tightly, almost as if he was afraid she'd wriggle away.

She breathed in his familiar smell of Ivory soap and warm skin. She'd learned in science class once that the sense of smell was the most connected to memory, and with her face buried in Drew's shirt, she knew that was true. Scenes of their relationship flashed before her eyes like a movie montage: their first date, the kisses they snuck in the back room of Ahoy, the Christmas they spent snowbound in Ithaca. She felt suddenly and unbelievably nostalgic for the relationship they once had. And she couldn't deny that it felt good to be held in Drew's arms again.

After a moment she stepped back and looked at him. His hair hung in the cute, shaggy way he liked to wear it, and his bright green eyes were full of affection.

"I'm so sorry," he said. "I made a huge mistake."

She didn't say anything. She just nodded and waited for him to go on.

He held out his arms in supplication. "I don't know what I was thinking. I must have been temporarily crazy or something. I mean, to not call you — and then to just decide to take that camp job. It was totally insane."

She nodded again, still silent.

He went on. "Can I plead insanity and declare myself at the mercy of the beautiful judge?" A small, hopeful smile flickered over his face. "I'm willing to be assigned to weeks of hard labor, including back rubs and foot massages. I promise to become fully rehabilitated and pay my debt to society through constant dedication and service to Ms. Lara Pressman."

Lara couldn't help but smile, even if she wished he wouldn't joke at a time like this. "Be serious," she told him, trying to remain stern. "You just vanished. You basically broke up with me by disappearing."

Drew sank back down onto one of the teak lounge chairs and gestured for her to come sit with him. "I don't know what got into me. I never meant to hurt you. You're the best thing that ever happened to me. Lara," he added softly, his voice full of longing. "Please give me another shot." His eyes were earnest and adoring.

Seeing him there, so familiar and beloved, made her realize just how much she'd missed him. It was more than she'd realized. As they gazed at each other, the hurt she'd felt began to evaporate like a drop of water in the sun. But even as he pulled her toward him and pressed her face into his neck, she couldn't push Marco out of her mind.

"So you came all the way to Maine to tell me this?" she asked. "You should have just called me in June. That would have made a lot more sense."

He traced his fingers lightly up and down her back and she shivered. "I came all the way to Maine to tell you that I know what I want now: I want us to be together. And that I think we should tell the rest of the family."

At that, she sat upright with a start. What was she doing

snuggling with him on the porch? What if Aunt Clare or someone came waltzing out and caught them?

She stood up and walked a few feet away, pretending to inspect the flowers Drew had brought her. She couldn't possibly wrap her mind around telling the Tuttle family about dating Drew, when up until five minutes ago she'd been convinced that their relationship was completely over. "These are really pretty," she said lamely.

"Seriously, Lara, listen," he said. "I quit the camp job because I wanted to spend time with you. So here I am. Don't you want to spend time with me?" He held out his arms, motioning for her to come back to him.

She pretended to be absorbed in the contemplation of the tightly curled rosebuds. She was so glad to see Drew; she really was — he meant so much to her! But then the little voice inside her head reminded her that Marco had begun to mean something to her, too.

"I'm glad you're here," she said honestly. "And I felt really bad about how we left things." She paused and gathered her courage for what she wanted to say next. "But I did some thinking, and now I'm pretty sure you were right to want to keep our relationship a secret." She tried to ignore Drew's look of surprise. "I mean, there are so many crazy family dynamics right now. Your mom and Aunt Trudy got in a fight yesterday about how to properly fold the guest room sheets, my stepdad is obsessing over this new grilling method he's discovered, which is really annoying Uncle Carr, and Greer's mom — well, let's just say that she needs to be physically restrained anytime a single male comes within twenty feet of her."

Drew couldn't help but laugh, and Lara felt encouraged. She was almost starting to believe her own excuses.

"I guess I just want to keep things as simple as possible for right now," she finished. *And I want to keep you and Marco as far away from each other as possible, too*, she thought. Because she couldn't just ditch Marco the moment Drew made his surprise appearance, could she? Well, technically she *could* — but she realized that she didn't want to. She had an amazing time when she was with Marco. And she still wasn't sure she forgave Drew for everything.

Drew nodded. "Okay, Lara," he said. "You've convinced me. As far as the Tuttles are concerned, we're cousins and nothing more."

"Stepcousins," Lara corrected.

"Right. Otherwise the way I'm going to kiss you would be really, really inappropriate."

Lara looked wildly around. "Here? Now? You want to kiss me? What about what we just talked about?"

Drew laughed. "Relax," he assured her. "I can wait until I catch you alone in your bedroom."

Lara smiled at him, and reached out and tucked one of his roses behind her ear. "So you'll pretend you brought these flowers for your mother, I guess," she said.

Drew nodded. "You better believe it. Maybe they'll get me out of doing the dishes tonight."

"Good luck with that." Lara smiled wryly. "She's pretty strict on the 'I made it so you clean it up' rule these days."

"Like you need to tell *me* that," Drew answered. "Don't forget she raised me."

And then, as if on cue, Clare appeared in the doorway with a pitcher of lemonade in one hand and a plate of cheese and crackers in the other.

"Who's hungry?" she asked, grinning at them both.

"Me," Lara said, going straight for the cheese. She figured if she ate about a pound of Brie, she might be able to quell the queasy feeling in her stomach that she just couldn't shake. She stuffed a cheese-smeared cracker into her mouth. If someone would have told her that she'd be kissing a hot Chilean guy one minute and her cute, sweet ex-boyfriend (or was it just boyfriend now? — she was so confused) the next, she never would have believed it. Not on her life.

"You must have been surprised to see my son appear on the porch," Clare said to Lara.

Lara, whose mouth was still full, nodded vigorously. *You have no idea*, she thought.

Jessica flipped through the glossy pages of one of Greer's magazines, half bored and half fascinated by the crap that people tried to pass off as fashion.

"Look, you guys," she said, pointing to one particularly egregious spread, in which a pouty-faced woman modeled a dress made out of what appeared to be blue and green feathers. "They've dressed this lady up like a freaking parrot, and they're saying this is the perfect outfit to wear on a cruise! I mean, come on! And look at those shoes she's wearing. Those are, like, eight-inch heels!"

But Lara and Greer hardly looked up from their spots on neighboring teak deck chairs. Lara was painting her toenails an electric blue, and Greer's nose had been buried in a book ever since she returned from a mani-pedi-facial appointment with her mother, Cassandra the cougar.

"Earth to my cousins," Jessica said again, but the girls just grunted at her.

Jessica frowned and looked at them closely. They'd both been acting strangely for the last couple of days. Witness, for example, the fact that Greer was reading an actual *book*, when she'd never before been seen reading anything longer than an article in *Vogue* or an instructional manual to her iPhone. And though electric blue toenails were pretty much par for the course for Lara, she was being really weird lately, too. It had started the moment Drew showed up; it was as if she was still so surprised to see him that she couldn't really be happy about it.

Feeling slightly ignored (and annoyed), Jessica turned back to the magazine. At least Connor would be coming over any minute. He would rescue her from boredom and grumpy cousins and take her somewhere fun, like the miniature golf course or the horse stables or *something*.

They hadn't exactly talked about the tensions that had arisen at the end of the romantic date that Jessica had planned, but they'd at least told each other that they loved each other face-to-face, and not just over the phone. As Greer would put it, they'd kissed and made up.

"How Downward Dog Can Change Your Life," read the headline she turned to next. *What in the world is a downward dog?* she wondered. Hesitantly, she asked her cousins, and was met with two exaggerated eye rolls.

"God, Jess, it's like you live in a cave or something. They *do* have yoga in Ithaca, don't they? It's a very basic yoga position," Greer groused. She leaned over and took a sip of the homemade lemonade that Clare Tuttle had brought them.

Jessica stuck her tongue out at Greer, even though it was immature, because she deserved it — but she'd gone back to her book again. "Well, soooooorry for asking," Jessica muttered.

She looked impatiently at her watch. Still ten more minutes until Connor was due to arrive, but as far as she was concerned, he couldn't show up quickly enough. Though relaxing on the big, sunny deck of their beach house should have been as pleasant as spending the day in a spa, her cousins were bumming her out.

Jessica finished off her own glass of lemonade and then lay back on the lounge chair. She closed her eyes, remembering the moment Connor had first texted her that he loved her. Her heart still skipped a beat whenever she thought of that.

With just a little effort, she'd managed to convince herself that Connor's rejection of her advances was just a minor bump in the road of an otherwise perfect relationship. He *loved* her, and no doubt he was going to prove it very soon.

She could feel the little smile forming on her lips, and she hoped that neither of her snarky cousins would say something snide about it. It wasn't her fault she had a great guy, was it?

Her happy musings were interrupted by the chirping of her cell phone: It was Connor. "Hey, babe," she said as soon as she answered.

"Hey," Connor replied. His voice sounded strange and far away. "Listen, I can't make it today after all. I'm sorry; can we reschedule?"

Jessica suppressed a momentary urge to fling the phone across the deck and down onto the beach. She was *not* in the mood to be rejected again. But she knew that Connor must have a good reason for canceling on her, so she tried to be nice about it. "Sure," she said. "But why?"

"Something came up over at the house here," he said, his voice still faint. "I'll call you later, babe. Love you."

When she hung up, she felt as grumpy as Greer looked. But Jessica refused to be the kind of person who felt sorry for herself. *And come to think of it, I'm not the kind of person who lets other people feel sorry for themselves, either*, she thought. And so she stood up and clapped her hands together firmly.

"All right, kids, this is ridiculous. Enough of the bad attitude. Look where we are! We're on a beautiful Maine beach in summer! And look at us! We're three gorgeous girls who have no excuse to lie around on a deck pouting!"

Her cousins gazed up at her, looking vaguely amused by her outburst. When neither said anything, though, Jessica went on. "I am making an edict! The edict goes like this: No Tuttle relation may waste a beautiful day by moping!"

"I'm not technically a Tuttle relation," Lara pointed out.

"Oh, shut up; you are, too," Jessica cried. "Your mom married Uncle Mike, which makes you a Tuttle whether you like it or not, so you'd better start liking it."

Greer raised one groomed brown eyebrow. "Looks like Jess is channeling some kind of positive-thinking-boot-camp-instructor thing."

"Damn straight," Jessica said, stomping her sandaled foot. "So get off your butts. Because we are going to Have. Some. Fun. First stop, the ice cream parlor, where you both will order something big and sweet and covered in sprinkles or else I will personally throw you into the ocean."

At that, Lara laughed. She looked over at Greer. "What do you say, cuz? The kid is pretty convincing."

Greer looked skeptical still, and Jessica blurted, "Like I said! Greer, get off your yoga-toned, fake-tanned, True Religion ass and put on those Mary-Kate Olsen shades of yours or *you will be sorry*."

Lara exploded in giggles, and even Greer began to smile. Slowly she stood up and placed the book on the table beside her. "I'll have you know," she said, grinning, "that my tan is 100 percent real by now. And Mary-Kate does not wear Chanel sunglasses; she wears Marc Jacobs."

Jessica nearly jumped up and down with excitement. "Oh, goody, we're all up and going," she cried, immediately dropping the drill sergeant approach. "It's my treat."

Linking arms, the cousins strolled down the path toward town, chattering about Jessica's inspiring temporary bossiness and whether Lara's electric blue toenails made her look edgy or like she had frostbite.

Pretty soon they found themselves outside Izzy's Ice Cream, a cute little beach shack painted in rainbow colors that looked almost edible itself. Flowers spilled out of window boxes and Izzy's fat old gray cat, Jellybean, lay purring in the sun.

"I'm going to get peppermint, mint chocolate-chip, and double-fudge mint," Jessica declared. "It's going to be a total mint explosion. A mint nuclear bomb!" She felt a little giddy.

Greer perused the menu that Izzy had tacked up outside his shop for the times when the ice cream line got really long. "He has sugar-free sorbet," she mused.

"Don't you dare," Jessica warned.

"She's right," Lara chimed in. "Bad moods can only be

truly countered by full-fat, 100 percent sugary ice cream. It's, like, a law of the universe or something."

"Fine," Greer sighed, giving in. "I'll have a coffee milk shake. And I'd better feel happier immediately, or else."

Jessica straightened her shoulders, standing up to her older cousin. "Hey! I make the threats around here!" she said and then immediately succumbed to a fit of giggles.

"Careful, there, Tiger," Lara cautioned, putting a hand on Jessica's shoulder. "You look like you might crack a rib."

When Jessica finally got her laughter under control, she looked around, beaming. She was feeling great, and she could tell that Greer and Lara were feeling a lot better, too. She was happily congratulating herself for her excellent idea when she saw something she'd never expected to see.

Connor.

Connor, who'd canceled on her because "something had come up," hurrying out of Izzy's with a double scoop of chocolate ice cream.

And another girl.

Jessica's jaw dropped, and Lara and Greer turned to see the cause of the rapid change in her demeanor.

"Oh, my," Lara whispered, and Jessica heard what sounded like a snarl coming out of Greer.

The girl's glossy red hair was tied back with a ribbon, and she wore a cute yellow sundress and a rope of pearls around her neck — like she was dressed up for a *date*, Jessica thought. She recognized the girl as Lily Fitzgerald, a friend of Connor's she'd met at Chace Warner's party back at the start of the summer. Connor had said that Lily was one of his best friends, and Jessica, of course, had taken him at his word. But did a guy really cancel on his girlfriend to hang out with someone who was just a *regular* friend? Jessica didn't think so.

Her mind felt suddenly foggy with confusion, and she had no idea what to do. She stood there dumbly, the money for the ice cream getting damp in her clenched fist.

"Go up and ask him, 'What the hell . . . ?'" Greer whispered, giving Jessica a little nudge.

Jessica felt her legs move woodenly forward. She saw Lily laugh and put her hand on Connor's arm, and she saw Connor smiling back at her.

Jessica couldn't believe it. She knew she had to find out what was going on. The trouble was, she couldn't seem to move anymore, and before she knew it, Connor and his "friend" had vanished down the steps to the beach.

14

The hot July sun beat down on Greer's shoulders as she stood on the Pebble Beach Athletic Club tennis court, clutching her racquet tightly with both hands as if she planned to use it as a weapon.

Which she did, in a way, she thought grimly. Because today was another lesson with her mother and Hunter, at whom she was still mad. Anger made Greer competitive and determined, often to good effect. (Her rage at her backstabbing classmate Brie Marshall, for example, had meant that Greer got the much better grade in AP History.) Today, of course, Greer's antagonist was Hunter; she'd be damned if she was going to let that blue-eyed Romeo show her up on the court, even if he had been hired to be her teacher.

Strong backhand, powerful serve, she thought to herself. *Strong backhand, powerful serve.* She repeated it enough so that it became a kind of mantra.

It was clear that Cassandra Hallsey was not feeling particularly competitive, however. She was too busy batting her eyelashes at Hunter and laughing at all of his lame jokes. (Greer wasn't really listening, but there was one about three blind mice and a bottle of tequila that prompted her mother to bray with laughter.) Cassandra was also wearing way too much makeup for a tennis lesson, Greer noted. With her flawless, perfectly powdered skin, dark eyeliner, and ruby lips, she looked like she was ready for a St. John photo shoot — not two hours on an asphalt court under a blazing summer sun.

Greer, on the other hand, had gone for the natural look — not that she didn't have makeup on, of course. She had applied numerous products, including concealer, sunscreen, blush, bronzer, and mascara. But the point was that she looked barefaced, as if she'd popped out of the shower looking just that beautiful.

"Remember that you want to aim the ball to the far side of the court," Hunter was instructing them. "You want to make your opponent run so he or she gets tired more quickly. By making them run, you are controlling their actions, which means that you're controlling the game itself."

"That strategy will appeal to my daughter, no doubt," Cassandra noted. "She's a bit of a control freak. Would you believe she tried to get me to change my outfit? She said my skirt was too short." And here Cassandra playfully stuck out a long, lovely leg and gave Hunter an eyeful. He looked admiringly at Cassandra's toned calves.

Ugh. Her mom was officially crossing the line. If she could just stop flirting with Hunter, who was young enough to be her son, and focus on the game, then they'd all be better off.

Maybe, Greer thought, she should have mentioned to her mother that she and Hunter had . . . well, *history*. Not that she'd divulge any details, of course, but the suggestion of, say, a kiss at a party might discourage her mother from practically shoving Hunter's face right in between her perky, augmented breasts.

Just then, Hunter served, lobbing an easy one in Greer's direction. Greer slammed it back to the far side of his court, just as he'd been suggesting. *Take that*, she thought fiercely. When Hunter returned the ball, Greer made a mad dash for it — even though it was heading for Cassandra — and spiked a low, mean shot that landed just inside the white line and then bounced away.

Greer one, Hunter zero, she thought.

Hunter pointedly did not praise her technique. Rather, he saved his compliments for Cassandra's shots, which were not half as strong or as well aimed as her daughter's. Cassandra tittered and giggled, lapping up the attention like a cat starved for milk. Or a *cougar*, Greer amended silently.

As the lesson progressed, it began to seem like Greer and Hunter were locked in a silent battle that neither would acknowledge to the other. She served as hard as she could, and he sent her shots flying back at her. Every time Hunter missed, Greer laughed inside, and every time she missed, she cursed. After half an hour, they were both sweaty and breathless, but the only communication between them was the occasional challenging glare.

Cassandra, naturally, was oblivious to it all, and she was having a fantastic time. "Oh, look how strong you are!" she'd cry when Hunter would return a ball. To which Hunter would say something sickening like, "Grace is as important as strength, and you, Ms. Hallsey, have the grace of a ballerina." Then he'd look over at Greer with a smug grin on his face and she would mime barfing onto the tennis court.

Because really, it was disgusting.

"Earth to Greer," her mother said, waving her racquet in front of Greer's face. "We've got to practice here! Our time's almost up and we need to get a few good volleys in. That *woman* — Monica, the one who still goes to *Aspen*? — is improving every day, and I'm not going to let a fishwife like her beat me."

Hunter idly bounced a ball on the other side of the court.

"Hunter, darling," Cassandra cried, "don't you think Greer needs to step up her game a bit?"

"Oh, I think she's pretty good at games in general," Hunter answered. He shot Greer a look as if to say, *Games like hiding in azalea bushes and trying to get me to hit on her cousin.*

Greer had had about enough of him. She picked up a tennis ball, tossed it into the air, and served it hard, right into Hunter's leg.

"Ouch," he said, reaching down to rub it.

"Oh, sorry," she said sweetly. "Maybe I'm not as good at games as you say."

Cassandra hurried across the court to make sure Hunter was okay. *She'll want to kiss his boo-boo and make it better,* Greer thought. She decided not to stick around to see if Hunter would let her, so she picked up her racquet and her bottle of Evian and headed toward the locker room, a jaunty swing in her step. Hunter was a jerk all right. But he was no match for Greer Hallsey.

15

Lara put the finishing touches on her outfit, adding a pair of white Lucite bangles to her wrist and a butterfly pin to her pink A-line dress, and then glanced in the mirror. Tonight she looked sort of like Audrey Hepburn in *Roman Holiday*, she thought. That was, if Audrey had blue fingernails and a habit of going shopping at the hippie stores on Haight-Ashbury.

"Groovy," Greer said in passing as she wandered into the living room.

Jokingly, Lara flashed her a peace sign, and then looked at the clock. It was 4:45. Fifteen minutes until she met Marco at the harbor, where they planned to sail two towns over for dinner at a little Italian place he liked. And, she thought ruefully, three hours and fifteen minutes until Drew planned to take her to dinner at Chez Paula in Pebble Beach.

Whatever had possessed her to say yes to two dates in one night, Lara had no idea. It was hardly characteristic of her — in part because she was usually more honest, and in part because she was usually disorganized and late and thus had difficulties with scheduling in general. The thought of juggling two boys like this unnerved her. But she'd said yes to them both without realizing the conflict, and once she did, it was too late to cancel.

But she couldn't help feeling a little excited, too. After all, how often did a girl have two cute guys clamoring for dates? Selfishly, Lara felt it was an opportunity not to be missed.

And, she reflected, she truly liked them both. She didn't want to have to choose between them. Not yet.

As she slid into Greer's Lexus (after loaning Sadie to Jessica for her date, Greer could hardly deny Lara her chance to drive it), she turned on the radio to the oldies station. It was a Crosby, Stills & Nash song, and she hummed it under her breath as she drove.

Marco was waiting on the deck of his boat, looking breathtakingly cute in a pair of docksiders, white shorts, and a navy-blue-and-white striped Oxford. For a second, when Lara saw him, she felt an overwhelming pang of guilt. He was so adorable, so sweet, and here she was, keeping this major secret from him. He had no idea about Drew.

Since when did I become such a two-timer? Lara asked herself.

The sails of Marco's boat had been unfurled, and they rustled behind him as if anxious to face the wind.

"Ahoy there, matey," she cried gaily, and then cringed. She could be such a goofball sometimes.

Marco grinned and helped her onto the boat. Then he planted a kiss right on her lips, which made her whole body warm with pleasure. "Howdy, sailor," he said, his dark eyes sparkling.

As they slid out of the harbor, heading south toward the town of Lincolnville, Marco handed Lara a glass of sparkling water and she sipped it gratefully.

"I think I could sail forever," she said, gazing down into the blue-green water. "I don't know why I have to live in Chicago, surrounded by pavement and high-rises and parking lots. I want to live on the ocean, in a little boat. I'll catch my food every morning, and I'll bathe in the salt water and all that good stuff."

Marco smiled and nodded thoughtfully; perhaps, Lara thought, he was imagining her diving naked into the bay for her morning bath.

"I know what you mean," Marco replied. "But then I

remind myself that dry land has things like movie theaters and museums and bookstores, all of which I'm pretty fond of."

Lara took another sip of water. "You have a point. Terra firma has thrift stores, too, which are some of my favorite places on earth."

As they moved into open water, the boat bobbed gently on the waves. Lara slid closer to Marco, and reached for his hand. "Thanks for taking me to dinner," she said.

"Don't thank me yet," he warned smilingly. "You might hate it."

"Impossible," she said. "I already know I like it."

He looked down at her with his deep, beautiful, dark eyes and then kissed her on the forehead. "You're cute."

She frowned playfully. "Cute? I prefer 'gorgeous,'" she teased, acting more confident than she felt.

"Well, you're that, too, obviously. I'm just trying to make sure you don't get a big head."

"Never," she assured him. "I have cousins to bring me down to earth whenever I get too full of myself." She thought fondly of Greer and Jessica. The former, especially, was always ready to take a person down a peg. For instance, there was the time Lara was trying to channel Joan Crawford in *Whatever Happened to Baby Jane?* and Greer told her that the shoulder pads in her 1940s-era suit made her look like a football player in drag.

Just then they hit a wave, and the salty spray splashed both of their faces, not to mention their clothes.

"Good thing I decided against the white dress," Lara commented, wiping the water from her eyes and wringing out the hem of her sheath. "That could have been scandalous."

"Too bad," Marco said. "I kind of like scandalous."

She poked him in the ribs and he laughed. Then he pointed ahead. "Look — the restaurant. Right there on the water."

Lara was instantly charmed by the homey little café that hugged the shore. White Christmas lights were draped festively along its porch, on which happy couples were enjoying plates of seafood risotto and spaghetti *con vongole*.

"It's perfect," she breathed. "And did I mention I'm starving?"

Over dinner they talked about their families and where they hoped to go to college. While Lara tried to save room for the next dinner she had coming up, everything was too delicious.

When the waiter finally removed their plates, she sat back and held her stomach in both hands. "Ohh," she said. "I must have eaten five dozen clams."

Marco waved the dessert menu in front of her. "But of course you have room for the tiramisu? Or the homemade cranberry gelato?"

Lara figured she could probably manage to stuff a few bites of dessert into her mouth — sugar, after all, was an essential part of her diet — but then she looked at her watch. She had only forty-five minutes until her date with Drew, which sent a little ripple of panic through her.

"Oh, I don't think so," she said, shifting nervously in her seat. "I'm really just too full. I think we should get going, don't you? Before it gets too dark?" When Marco didn't reply right away, she continued breathlessly. "I mean, I know you're an experienced sailor and everything, but being on the ocean at night makes me kind of nervous. It's all that dark, deep water business. I keep thinking that maybe the Loch Ness Monster or Jaws or something might be swimming around beneath me. And maybe he hasn't had as big a dinner as we did, so he's really hungry, and he thinks that a girl from Chicago sounds like just the ticket to fill him up. You know? I mean, wow, I guess I'm not ready to live on a boat after all!" Lara was surprised at her ability to lie this way.

Marco gave her an odd look and she understood that she was babbling. But it was extremely important that they leave, *right now*, and if they didn't, she was going to have to start feigning a headache or a sudden case of narcolepsy or something.

But Marco signaled the waiter for the check, and quickly enough they were heading back to Pebble Beach. Lara wanted to cuddle up to him as she had earlier, but she was just too jittery.

Back in the harbor, he kissed her good night tenderly, and she nearly didn't get off the boat. She almost just blew off the date with Drew entirely. But she didn't. She disentangled herself unwillingly from Marco's strong, brown arms and headed back to Greer's car.

"Thanks again — I'll call you," she yelled to Marco, who waved and blew her a kiss.

"Try the choucroute," Drew urged Lara. "It's a house specialty."

She looked at him blankly. He'd dressed up for their date, and he looked very handsome in his vintage sport coat and skinny tie. He looked a little like a young Paul McCartney, in fact, back when he was in the Beatles, except that Drew was much better-looking. He'd even given her another bouquet of flowers. As she'd thanked him, the feel of Marco's kisses still lingering on her lips, she'd felt like one of the worst, most deceitful people in the world.

Lara looked at him in bafflement. "What in the world is choucroute? It sounds like a fancy crouton." *And a single crouton is about all I can bear to eat right now*, she thought.

Drew folded his hands over his menu. "It's a long-simmered combination of sausages, smoked meats, and sauerkraut," he informed her. "It's a traditional dish of the

Alsatian region of France, which is where Paula of Chez Paula is from."

Lara glanced up to see a small, fifty-something woman with long, gray braids and a long, white apron smiling at Drew.

"That's her," he said, waving. "Her daughter used to babysit me, and she'd always feed me choucroute after the beach."

Even the *sound* of choucroute made Lara feel full to bursting. "I was sort of leaning toward the salad," she said meekly.

He threw up his hands. "Women!" he cried theatrically. "Always dieting."

Lara nodded, happy to be offered the calorie-restricting excuse. "It *is* bathing suit season, after all!" she said brightly.

After they ordered, Drew filled her in on the various exploits of his summer campers: There had been the requisite water balloon wars, food fights, and pantie raids, of course. There'd been one kid who liked to stuff spaghetti noodles up his nose and another who refused to wear his bathing trunks, insisting, instead, on swimming in his footy pajamas. "And don't get me started on the kid who thought he could talk to the animals just like Dr. Dolittle," Drew warned.

Lara giggled at his stories, and she remembered again

how much fun they'd had last summer. If there was one person who could always be counted on to make her laugh, it was Drew. Even his purposely lame jokes — like the elephant series ("Why did the elephant sit on the marshmallow? So he wouldn't fall into the hot chocolate!", etc.) — were funny, just because he delivered them with such obvious pleasure.

Even though they'd been talking on the phone nearly every day up until their fight, it seemed like so much had happened since then. Lara had become obsessed with Flannery O'Connor's short stories, and was eager to share with Drew the plots of the weirder ones. Drew had finally learned how to drive a stick shift after his older brother, Jordan, had bet him twenty dollars that he wasn't coordinated enough to master it. They compared notes on the movies they'd seen and rented, and debated whether or not *Pirates of the Caribbean* was (a) a good *bad* movie, (b) a good *good* movie, or (c) a bad *bad* movie. Lara voted for (c) while Drew held out for (a).

Drew devoured his giant plate of choucroute, while Lara ate about three leaves of lettuce and one cherry tomato. When they'd finished, Drew reached across the table for her hand. "I'm so glad we're back together again," he said.

So we are together? Lara wondered, feeling both happy and confused. Where did that leave things with Marco?

She had never dated two guys before, and she'd never imagined that she could like two different people equally. As night finally descended over the streets of Pebble Beach, Lara felt full of both food and anxiety. She wondered how long she could possibly keep this situation up. That annoying little voice in her head warned her that it wouldn't be for very long.

16

The fourteenth of July — Bastille Day in France, and Chace Warner's birthday in Pebble Beach — dawned hazy and hot, and the humidity did no favors to Jessica's hair or her mood. Greer had solved the first problem with a dab of Kérastase Lait Nutri-Sculpt, which restored Jessica's blonde locks to their normal smoothness, but the two cousins' attempts to cheer Jessica up were not improving her gloomy outlook.

Lara offered her a bite of her very favorite candy bar — dark chocolate with pieces of crystallized ginger — but Jessica shook her head. She felt like she'd lost her taste for sweets ever since she'd spotted Connor coming out of Izzy's Ice Cream with another girl.

"I mean, just who is this Lily person anyway?" she fumed for what was probably the millionth time. "If she's BFFs with Connor, how come I've never hung out with her? Is he trying to keep her a secret from me?"

Greer disappeared into their shared bedroom for a moment and then returned to the living room where Lara and Jessica were spread out on the soft taupe couches. All the adults were off at the beach, and the house was quiet.

"Here," Greer said firmly, holding out a laptop so sleek and tiny it could have almost fit in her little royal blue Banana Republic satchel. "Time for a little detective work."

When Jessica looked at her blankly, Greer sighed and logged onto Facebook. After another moment, she was on Connor's page.

"You're friends with Connor on Facebook?" Jessica asked incredulously.

"Of course, dummy," Greer answered. "I'm friends with everybody. Because personally I prefer electronic friends to actual ones. Actual ones are always calling you up and wanting you to do things, when really all a person wants is to be left alone."

Jessica looked at her quizzically. "I don't want to be left alone."

"Me, either," Lara piped in.

"Well, whatever," Greer said dismissively. "One man's meat is another man's poison."

Lara and Jessica shared a quizzical look as Greer went on. "The point, Jessica, is to find out what Lily has posted on Connor's wall and to see if it's at all incriminating."

"Did you learn this tactic watching *CSI*?" Lara queried jokingly.

"Please," Greer said, her eyes glued to the screen. "Like I watch that trash."

Jessica leaned over her cousin's shoulder as Greer scrolled down Connor's page. She was not at all pleased to see plenty of little pictures of Lily popping up, signaling the girl's public messages to Connor. "Happy birthday, sweetie," said one, from several months ago. Another said, "Hope you feel better" and was signed XOXOXO.

Jessica frowned deeply. She'd seen some of these posts before, but she'd never thought twice about them. She'd assumed they were completely innocent. Now, however, they took on a different tone entirely. What did Lily mean, exactly, when she called Connor "sweetie"?

Jessica read farther down on the page, finding more messages that seemed just a little too affectionate. "If her public messages are that lovey-dovey, what do you think her private e-mails to him might say?" she wondered.

"I know a hacker," Greer said mildly, "if that's the direction you want to go."

Jessica shook her head, though there was a tiny part of her that was curious. "No," she said, "definitely not."

Lara sat up and plucked a shiny Granny Smith from the giant fruit bowl that Aunt Trudy kept in the living room "to encourage healthy eating and the consumption of fiber." Trudy had a thing about fiber.

"I think you need to be careful, Jessica," Lara said, taking a big bite of the apple. "Connor is a really sweet guy, and I don't think you want to jump to any conclusions about his relationship with Lily."

Jessica was still staring at Lily's wall posts and wondering why it had never occurred to her that Lily might have a thing for Connor. Or that Connor might have a thing for Lily.

"Hello? Hey, Jessica," Greer said, waving a hand in front of her face. "As much as I hate to admit it, seeing as how I prefer to assume the worst about people, I think Lara has a point. Connor is *not* like Liam, that player brother of his. He's a good guy, and he really cares about you. I'm sure he had a perfectly good reason for bailing on you to take Lily to ice cream."

Jessica fell back against the cocoa-colored shantung throw pillows and moaned. "When you put it that way, you know perfectly well that it sounds terrible. Bailing on me to take Lily to get ice cream!"

Greer reached and gently touched Jessica's shoulder.

"I didn't mean it to sound like that. I really do think Connor must have had a really good reason for doing what he did."

"Yeah, and you should just talk to him," Lara said, her mouth full of apple. "Find out what the reason is."

Jessica nodded slowly. She knew her cousins weren't only trying to make her feel better — they were making actual sense. "You're right," she sighed. "I'll talk to him tonight. He said he'd meet me at Chace's party."

Greer rolled her eyes. "Why can't anyone else throw a party in this town?" she asked. "That guy is such a loser."

"Actually he's kind of nice," Lara said. "When he's not being drunk and stupid, that is. I ran into him the other day at Ahoy."

"And he has a really good house for parties," Jessica pointed out, already feeling better about the evening's plans.

Lara leaned over to a side table where the multiple remote controls were gathered in a confusing cluster. "Does anyone have any idea which one turns on this giant TV? I want to watch Animal Planet."

Jessica reached out and poked her with her toe. "Don't change the subject! We're still talking about tonight." She still wanted to talk about her fears about Connor, but she didn't want to sound like a whiner. So she said, "I want to know what you guys are planning on wearing."

"Hmmm," Greer said. "I'm going to guess that Lara's going to go for something like Marilyn Monroe meets Sofia Coppola."

Lara grinned. "I like the sound of that. Maybe you can help me put something together?"

Greer nodded. "Of course. And you, too, Jessica. We're not going to let you go to Chace's in a T-shirt and athletic shorts, no matter how comfortable you say they are. And I am banning any mention of your Keds, even the supposedly cute ones with the daisies all over them."

Jessica giggled and reached for an apple herself. "No Keds!" she cried. "And I promise to wear a skirt to Chace's." She bit into the apple and smiled. "As long as you let me borrow one."

"Of course," Greer said. "We'll find you a skirt that'll make Connor Selden forget Lily even exists."

"That sounds like a very good plan," Jessica said, and took another big bite.

Chace Warner certainly was enthusiastic about his birthday and about the country of France, Greer thought, eyeing the red-white-and-blue bunting draped over the front of his house, the HAPPY BIRTHDAY balloons tethered in great clumps here and there on the lawn, and the caterers wearing Louis XVI wigs. Who really celebrated Bastille Day, anyway?

She reached out to a passing tray of vodka tonics and grabbed one. Greer had to hand it to Chace: His taste was gauche, but he'd spared no expense in making his birthday party one to remember.

Naturally he tried to hit on her again, complimenting her on her Julie Haus romper and Joan & David heels ("You look like you just stepped off a runway," he said, which was not a particularly original come-on line as far as Greer was concerned). And Greer, rather than cutting him down, politely laughed and excused herself. *No sense in making the host feel bad,* she thought. Chace might be a flawed person, but no one could say he wasn't extremely generous with his food and drink. She would consider her friendliness to him as a kind of birthday present.

Greer spotted Lara near the pool, engrossed in a conversation with a hot guy who looked like he might be Latino. *That must be the famous Marco,* Greer thought, inspecting him closely. He had thick dark hair, strong brown arms, and a killer smile. In that instant, Greer understood Lara's attraction to him completely. Greer didn't think Jessica would get it, though, especially when she thought Lara was dating her brother. So she hoped for Lara's sake that the younger girl never spotted them.

She moved through the crowd, nodding hello to familiar faces. She saw a girl who worked at Ahoy with Lara, and the freckled twins whose father owned the movie theater. Without acknowledging it to herself, she was hoping to find Hunter somewhere in the crowd. They hadn't talked since their fiery exchange on the tennis court, and Greer had spent more time thinking about him than she liked to admit.

Probably her mother had been thinking about him, too, which was a mortifying thought. Thanks to Hunter's flirtations, Cassandra probably believed he had a crush on her. And for all Greer knew, he did, and that instead of the "Take me home to Mom" person he claimed to be, Hunter was actually a "Take me home to your mom's bed" kind of person.

But she told herself that couldn't be true, because if it were, Cassandra wouldn't be able to shut up about it. And Cassandra hadn't said anything, even though she and Greer had gone out to dinner together — something they *never* did in Manhattan — just last night. Instead her mother had spent most of the time drinking champagne and talking about some antiaging compound that apparently made mice live 200 percent longer.

Greer took a big gulp of her vodka tonic and helped herself to a few chocolate-covered strawberries. She didn't know why it was so hard to find a trustworthy guy — she thought her objective for the summer was a simple one. How wrong she was.

Thinking about the goals she and her cousins had set — the list of which she still kept hidden in her purse — made Greer realize that she hadn't seen Jessica at all tonight. Greer imagined that maybe she'd already managed to find Connor and patch things up with him, and now she was off achieving her summer goal with him. Naturally she approved, but if Jessica really was in some dark bedroom, surrendering her virginity to Connor, then it was a shame Greer had spent an hour getting Jessica ready for the party. She'd applied her makeup, fixed her hair, and dressed her in a fabulous peasant miniskirt that was the perfect mix of sweet and sexy. Lara had added a nice silver chain necklace ("From a church rummage sale! It was fifty cents," she'd chirped), and Jessica had looked undeniably beautiful.

Well, Greer thought, *if Connor's busy undoing all of our hard work, so be it. I hope they're happy.*

She was contemplating the buffet table, which was stacked high with all sorts of goodies, when she saw Hunter over by the badminton net. She banished all thought of nourishment and went striding over to him, her hazel eyes blazing.

He didn't see her until she was right in front of him, waving her manicured finger in his face. "You have some nerve, Hunter Brown," she spat. "Hitting on my mother like that!"

Hunter abandoned his normally cool demeanor and moved her finger away brusquely. "You seem to like playing games so much, Greer," he said snidely, "you inspired me to play one of my own."

"So you flirt with my mother just to piss me off?" she demanded.

Hunter allowed himself a little smirk. "Something like that," he said. "Though you know, your mom *is* pretty cute."

Greer was so annoyed that she was at an utter loss for words. This sudden muteness was very uncharacteristic of her, and it made her even angrier. She decided to go — to leave him standing like an idiot with his fake grin and his perfect teeth. And so she turned sharply away, dismissing him with a wave of her hand — and that was when one of the four-inch statement heels she was wearing snapped in two.

She let out a little shriek as she fell, but before her body made contact with the bright green grass of Chace's lawn, Hunter reached out and caught her in his arms.

"Whoa, there," he said into her ear. "Don't ruin that hot outfit of yours."

Greer gazed up into his ice blue eyes. She felt relieved, turned on, and mad all at the same time. His arms were still around her, and she loved how they felt, even though she still wanted to push him away. Slowly she disentangled herself from him and reached down to remove the broken shoe.

"Three hundred dollars and they're about as sturdy as toothpicks," she muttered angrily.

Hunter chuckled. "That's why you'll only ever see me in flats," he joked.

She reached out and swatted his arm. "I'm still mad at you," she said, "so don't try to be funny and charming."

His grin vanished. "I'm still mad at you, then." He

picked up a beer from the grass and looked at it. "I *think* this is mine," he said, and then took a sip.

"Disgusting," Greer said.

"Do you still believe in cooties?" Hunter responded.

Greer sniffed. "No, but I believe in cytomegalovirus and all the other horrible things you can contract by drinking someone else's beverage."

But what about when you kiss someone? a voice in Greer's head taunted.

They simply looked at each other for a while, each daring the other to break the stare. Then Chace came toward them with a bottle of whiskey in one hand and a hot dog in the other. "Lessss do birthday shotsss!" he bellowed drunkenly.

Hunter laughed. "Not for me, I'm driving," he said. "But thanks."

Greer shook her head. "I don't do whiskey." Hunter poked her. "But thanks," she added, trying to sound sincere.

"Whan sssome hot dog?" He held the frankfurter under Greer's nose, which she wrinkled in distaste. She shook her head, barely refraining from adding, *And I don't do ground-up pig parts, either.*

"Ssssuit yerssself," Chace slurred, and went off to find guests who were more enthusiastic about wieners and whiskey shots.

She and Hunter were alone again, and the air between them seemed to crackle with tension.

"Maybe we should go somewhere and talk," Hunter suggested.

Greer shrugged as if she couldn't care less what they did. "All right."

She followed him into Chace's giant house, past the den full of kids dancing to Jay-Z, through the big gleaming kitchen, and up the creaky back stairs. She remembered walking up these very stairs the night she'd met Hunter. She'd been just trying to have a little fun that night — how was she to know it would all get so complicated?

Upstairs they stopped in front of a familiar door. "Just to talk," Hunter assured her, motioning for her to go inside.

Greer saw the same gray quilt, the same silly William Wegman poster of two dogs posing by a patch of sunflowers. She went and sat down on the bed, and, after shutting the door behind him, Hunter came to join her.

"Still mad," she told him, and turned away stubbornly.

"Me, too," he replied.

They were quiet for a while, and then Greer felt Hunter's gentle fingers on her neck. She closed her eyes as he began to rub the tense muscles there, and pretty soon she wasn't thinking about how mad she was at all — she was thinking only of how good it felt.

"Mmmm," she said, without meaning to.

She could almost hear Hunter smiling. "You like that?" he whispered. Then he bent his head and began to kiss her throat, and she let out a little moan of pleasure.

She resisted for another few moments, and then she unclenched her fingers and let her hands run through his hair. She pulled his face up so she could kiss him. Their tongues met, and Hunter wrapped his arms tight around her waist.

She couldn't be mad at him, not when he made her feel like she was floating, just by kissing her.

As he reached for the buttons of her romper, she told herself that all was forgiven. She felt her skin flush with heat and her heartbeat coming hard and fast in her chest. And when Chace's birthday fireworks began to explode outside the window in all the colors of the rainbow, it was almost as if she'd summoned them herself, just by lying back in Hunter's arms.

"'Frankly Mr. Shankly, this position I've held . . .'" Lara sang, and then stopped. She waited to see if Marco knew which lines came next.

"'It pays my way and it destroys my soul,'" Marco replied effortlessly. "I'm telling you, I know 99 percent of the Smiths' songs. You can't defeat me in this game."

She sighed theatrically, fairly convinced that he was right. She'd tried every single Morrissey line she could remember, and Marco had known all of them. And the funny thing was, he said he didn't even like the Smiths that much. He said he was more of a Rolling Stones/Clash/ Replacements kind of guy.

They were sitting on a bench underneath a lilac tree in Chace Warner's giant backyard, sipping beers and watching the tanned summer people mingle and chatter. Lara had directed Marco to this particular bench because she wanted to keep a low profile. After all, she didn't want Jessica to see her flirting with Marco — and needless to say, she *certainly* didn't want Drew to come upon the two of them. But he'd been asleep when she left the house, and his mom, Clare, said she'd be shocked if her son woke up long enough to kick off his shoes, let alone get up and go out to a party.

So while Lara considered her position to be relatively safe, she didn't really want to parade around holding Marco's hand. There was no sense in tempting fate. Even sitting in this out-of-the-way place, her stomach still fluttered queasily with nerves.

She glanced over at Marco's profile. He hadn't shaved that morning, so there was a dark, sexy shadow along his jawline. His pants were appealingly rumpled — he'd been sailing, he said, and hadn't had time to change — and his feet were tan in their faded black flip-flops. As Greer would say, he looked positively edible.

"I could probably stump you with Ashlee Simpson lyrics," Lara teased, giving him a nudge.

Marco laughed. "Hardly. For one thing, I'm sure you don't know any of them yourself. And for another thing, doesn't ol' Ashlee do a good job of stumping herself? What about that time on *Saturday Night Live* —"

"When she started to sing the wrong song," Lara squealed. "How embarrassing would *that* be?"

"Very," Marco said. "It's yet another reason I'll never be a teen pop star."

Lara took a sip of her beer and decided that she was lucky her life was anonymous enough that there was very little chance of public humiliation. Sure, she'd made a fool of herself a few times — like the night at karaoke when she decided that she could channel Sir Mix-A-Lot doing "Baby Got Back." Or the time she went to school wearing one brown boot and one black one because she'd been so tired when she got dressed in the morning that she couldn't even see straight.

But those were minor goofs, the kind of screwups that only she would remember. As far as cosmic mistakes went, it was so far, so good.

But you're tempting fate, she told herself, thinking of her dual dates. She was busy reassuring herself that everything would work out fine when her breath caught in her throat.

She spotted Drew coming onto the deck, peering intently into the crowd.

Clearly looking for her.

Immediately her limbs began to tingle with adrenaline, and she didn't know whether she ought to laugh, cry, or just run away entirely. Everything had suddenly gotten *much* more complicated.

Warily, she stood up, gesturing vaguely toward the party crowd near the pool. "You know," she said, hoping Marco couldn't hear the rising panic in her voice. "I think we need more drinks. I'll go get them."

"I'll come, too," Marco said, also rising.

She shook her head firmly. "No, you stay here and relax. I'll be back in a little bit. There are probably a few people I should say hi to."

Before he could protest, she walked quickly away, losing herself in the throng of people in front of the buffet. She grabbed a brownie — she was going to need a serious injection of sugar to buoy her spirits — and then went to join Drew on the deck.

"I can't believe you came!" she cried, pulling him back into the living room and out of Marco's line of vision. "Your mom said you were in for the night."

Drew reached out and gave her a big hug. "I didn't want to miss a chance to hang out with you," he replied. "Or to miss this kid's crazy party! I hear he's going to have fireworks. Remember last year, on the Fourth of July, when Richard let us close early to watch the fireworks down on the pier?"

Lara nodded mutely, remembering how they'd kissed as the sky exploded with sparkling colors above them. Everything had been so much simpler then, she thought. She and Drew hadn't fought, and she'd never met a sweet, funny guy who shared a striking resemblance to Gael García Bernal.

Drew said, "Come on, let's go outside. I want to see who's here."

"Oh, no one exciting," Lara said breezily. "Why don't we just sit down in here?" She pointed to a deep leather couch a few feet away. One end was empty; on the other end, a couple in matching Abercrombie T-shirts was doing some serious tongue-wrestling.

"What, you don't want to be seen with me or something?" Drew asked, only sounding half-joking.

Lara forced out a laugh. "Don't be silly! Of course I want to be seen with you. It's just —"

"Our parents aren't here, you know," Drew reminded her, gently tucking a strand of hair behind her ear. "It's one thing to be all strange and secretive around them, but here, at this frat guy's house? I don't get it."

Lara bit her lip, not sure how to respond. "I don't know," she said eventually. "I guess once you're used to keeping something a secret, it's hard to be open about it."

Drew did not seem convinced by this excuse, so she tried another tactic. "What if we went somewhere private for a little while?" she said as seductively as she could.

But instead of nodding enthusiastically, Drew shot her a strange look. "You're acting kind of weird," he told her.

She looked down at the ground in shame; she knew he was right. But she really did want to be alone with him, in part because she didn't want him and Marco to meet, and in part because every time she saw Drew she was reminded of how much she cared for him. How sweet his kisses were. How much she loved gazing into those green, green eyes of his.

"I have to go to the bathroom," she blurted. "Stay here. I'll be back in a minute." As she hurried away, she turned back. "There'll probably be a line, so if I take a while, don't get nervous! I didn't fall in or anything!" She hoped he would smile at her, but he just looked at her quizzically.

She ducked farther into the house, then slipped out the front door, went around the side of Chace Warner's garage, and jogged out to the backyard, where she reappeared in front of Marco, breathless and smiling nervously.

Marco looked pointedly at her empty hands. "I thought you were bringing us drinks," he said.

Lara's heart sank. She was such an idiot. She remembered now why she never lied — because she was horrible at it. "Um," she said, hesitating. "Um, the line was really long, and I got impatient, and really, I think I'm buzzed already, aren't you?"

She smiled at him but Marco didn't smile back. When he spoke, his voice had lost all trace of warmth. "If you don't want to be seen with me, or if you don't want me to meet your friends, then I don't really know what you're doing here with me at all."

Lara felt a pang of horror. *Oh, no.* She reached out to touch him but he scooted down the bench away from her. "It's not that at all," she said desperately.

"Then what is it?" he asked.

But she didn't really have an answer for him. What could she say? *Sorry, but my other sort-of boyfriend just showed up?* She put her fingers on her temples and rubbed them. "I don't think I feel well," she whispered.

Marco's chivalrous manner returned immediately. "Are you okay? I'll walk you home."

She shook her head. "No, thank you. You stay and enjoy the party. I'll talk to you soon." And with that, she turned around and left, leaving Marco on the bench under the lilac with no one to talk to and no fresh beer to drink.

She found Drew where she'd left him in the living room. He was staring unseeingly at the TV, which was tuned, for some reason, to a cooking show.

"Hey," she said softly.

He turned to her. "Hey yourself."

She offered him a piece of the brownie — her second — that she'd swiped from the buffet table. He shook his head.

"You know," he said, "I really am sick of the secrecy. I think it's time people knew."

Lara looked at him pleadingly. "Can we talk about this later?" she asked. "I actually don't feel so great. It must have been a bad piece of sushi or something."

Drew's brow furrowed with concern. "Do you need to go home?"

She nodded. "Yes, but you stay here. I'm just going to go home and go to bed." She leaned over to kiss him good night, and then she fled the party as fast as she could.

Chace Warner, who was standing on the front porch holding a fistful of sparklers, bade her a drunken farewell. She waved to him as, one by one, the sparklers fizzled out in his hands.

She felt a little like a sparkler herself — briefly shining and bright, and then cold and cheap and useless. *You've gotten yourself into a real mess this time, Lara Frances Pressman*, she thought. And then she disappeared into the cool July night.

NOT UP 2 PARTY – SORRY – T2UT. XOXO.

Jessica stared at her phone in disbelief. Connor was bailing on Chace's party? It was totally unlike him to miss a chance to hang out with all of his friends. Connor was the kind of guy who'd go to a party even if he had mono, chicken pox, or any number of communicable diseases. She knew for a fact that he'd checked himself out of the hospital AMA (against medical advice) with a broken foot, just so he could make it to his older brother's graduation bash. ("And I even danced once I got there!" he'd told Jessica gleefully.)

She sighed and glanced down at the outfit that she and her cousins had spent nearly two hours assembling: a sleek, fitted cotton Calvin Klein tank paired with a flirty little ruffled skirt, Nine West strappy platforms, Lara's necklace, and the multicolored bangles that she'd gotten on sale (for three dollars!) at Forever 21. Her hair had been pulled back into a messy, effortless-looking twist (which had naturally taken plenty of effort to perfect), with wispy golden tendrils framing her face.

It was such a shame to waste all that fashion, she thought. Without Greer and Lara to help her, Jessica was fairly certain she'd never look this put together again.

NOT GOING IF UR NOT GOING, Jessica texted back. U BETTER HAVE A GOOD EXCUSE THO.

Her mother breezed by in the hall, carrying a tray of drinks for the grown-ups, who were gathered down on the beach. "Aren't you supposed to be gone already?" she chirped.

Jessica didn't bother to answer. Instead she got up, squared her shoulders, and strutted down to the garage. She wasn't going to sit at home and mope about missing Chace Warner's birthday. She was going to find out exactly why Connor didn't feel up to the party.

Twenty minutes later, she was parked outside his house in her mom's Volvo, feeling sort of like a creepy stalker. But she told herself that she was only doing this to make sure he was okay. What if he'd suffered a concussion while surfing that rendered him permanently disinterested in soirees and get-togethers? What if he'd gotten sunburned so badly he had temporarily lost the use of his legs? What if — and she hated herself for thinking this, but she couldn't help it — what if he'd gotten a call from Lily and had decided to spend time with her instead?

She tried to shake that last unpleasant notion from her mind by turning on the radio. All the stations were set to oldies and easy listening. Jessica had to search around to find a DJ who was playing songs that weren't twice as old as she was.

As the familiar sound of a Beyoncé number piped through the speakers, Jessica leaned back and waited. Darkness had fallen, and the windows of Connor's house glowed warm and welcoming. She saw the silhouette of a cat in one, and the outline of a big houseplant in another. She watched as a shadowy figure, probably Connor's dad, passed from one room on another holding what looked like the handle of a broom.

Yes, she was definitely a creepy stalker.

Just as she was getting ready to start the car and go home, she saw Connor emerge from the front door. Judging by the bounce in his step, it wasn't sickness or a concussion that was keeping him from the party. She watched as he got into his convertible Carmen Ghia and pulled out of the driveway. She ducked down in the front seat as he passed by.

Feeling highly suspicious, she followed him, keeping what she hoped was a good distance from his vehicle (her experience tailing someone was limited to watching episodes of *Law & Order*). He drove into town, past Ahoy, where a party was going full force, past Izzy's, past crowds of people enjoying the summer evening. Finally, Connor turned into the parking lot of Dave's Super Supermarket.

Grocery shopping? Jessica thought. *He blows off a party to go grocery shopping?*

She considered following him inside the cool, fluorescent-lit store, but then decided to stay outside. After all, it was one thing to pursue him in a car, in the dark, and another entirely to trail him up and down the soup aisle.

When he reappeared five minutes later, he carried a brown paper sack, the contents of which she couldn't guess. *It had better not be some more ice cream for Lily*, she thought bitterly.

And so once again she tailed him along the quiet Maine streets as the moon rose in the sky and the bats began to circle in the air. In the distance, she heard the boom of fireworks. She was so engrossed in her pursuit that she paid no attention to where Connor was heading. So when he stopped his car and got out, she was shocked to see that it was in front of her very own house.

Thinking quickly, she kept on driving for a little while, and then she circled back and pulled into her driveway.

"Hey you," she called, seeing him mount the steps to her front door, "what are you doing here?"

He turned and greeted her with a giant smile. "Hey yourself," he answered. "Where'd you come from?"

"I just got home from . . . I went to Ahoy to see if Drew was there," she lied.

"Cool," he said, obviously seeing nothing out of the ordinary in that. "Well, when you said you weren't going to go to Chace's party, either, I realized I'd have the chance to see you alone. Which was what I wanted in the first place. I brought you something."

She took the paper sack from his outstretched arms, and looked inside to see a box of Hostess doughnuts (her favorite guilty pleasure) and a beautiful bouquet of delphiniums and freesias (her absolute favorite flowers). "Oh," she gasped, "they're wonderful!"

He was smiling at her so happily that it erased all doubts about Lily from her mind. No guy could be this sweet and still be a cheat, she told herself.

"You're the best!" she said, meaning it.

Connor hugged her tightly, then took a step back and shrugged. "What can I say? I am a very excellent boyfriend. Possibly the very best there is anywhere," he said pompously.

"Oh, I don't know," she answered with mock serious-ness. "You might have to show up with some serious jewelry to earn that title. Have you seen that crystal necklace my brother got Lara for Christmas?"

Connor put his hands over his heart. "What, that gor-geous ring I got you from the gumball machine the other week wasn't enough?"

She swatted his arm playfully, and then motioned him to come inside. "Let's go up and sit on the deck," she said, and he took her hand and squeezed it.

Thankfully the porch was empty, and so they cuddled together in one of the big lounge chairs. The cool breeze sighed through the beach grasses. Way out in the water, they could see the twinkling lights of ships sailing through the night to far-off destinations.

"So how come you didn't want to go to the party?" Jessica asked, burying her face in his neck. He smelled like sunshine and soap. "You said you'd see me tomorrow."

He kissed the top of her head. "I just didn't feel like going, but I didn't want to stop you from having fun." He pulled her closer to him. "But now we can just be together without a lot of crazy people running around. We couldn't do that at Chace Warner's house. It'd be like try-ing to have an intimate moment at Maine's version of the Playboy Mansion."

She looked up and met his steel-gray gaze. "I really

love you, you know," she whispered. She decided not to ask him about the sex thing tonight — to, for once, just let her worries go.

Connor's smile was so big she thought his face would crack. "I love you, too," he replied.

And then they didn't talk anymore, because they were making out like two teenagers in love. Which was exactly what they were.

Greer shoved her wedge espadrille sandals into her locker at the Pebble Beach Athletic Club and then slipped on her tennis shoes. It was too bad one couldn't play tennis in heels, she thought, because sneakers were so boring — even her pearly John Paul Gaultier ones, which she'd snagged for a mere eighty dollars at the Barney's sample sale.

At least she'd started to enjoy her tennis lessons, though. Ever since her hookup with Hunter at Chace Warner's birthday party, things had been going much more smoothly on — and especially off — the court. Her backhand was much better, and her mother's tendency to swat the ball *into* the net instead of over it had almost been completely conquered.

Of course, Cassandra was still drooling over Hunter and every other male under the age of fifty, but Greer had mostly learned to ignore it. *She just wants to have a little fun*, Greer would remind herself whenever she saw her mother flirting. *She just wants to have a little fun*. It had become a kind of mantra.

And her mother did seem to be in better spirits, which was nice. When Cassandra wasn't being obnoxious, Greer actually enjoyed getting coffee or doing yoga with her. And when she *was* being obnoxious, she just focused on tuning it out; she told herself that her mother wasn't her problem.

Greer attributed her uncharacteristic peace of mind to sun, sea, and . . . *sensuality*, to be delicate about her relationship with Hunter. Not that Greer and Hunter spent all their time horizontal — far from it. Just last week they'd bicycled to a neighboring town, where they'd traded in their bikes (temporarily, that is) for a couple of horses so they could take an oceanside trail ride. Greer, who was an accomplished equestrian but a terrible cyclist — after all, New York City was hardly prime biking territory — had done very well cantering down the beach on her bay gelding, but had managed to wipe out twice on her little Schwinn. Hunter had the opposite skill set, and it was an unending source of amusement for Greer to watch him bouncing up and down in his saddle, clutching his mount's mane in a desperate attempt to keep from sliding off. When he let go of his horse just long enough to shake his fist in mock anger at her, she nearly howled with laughter.

And two days ago, they'd driven Sadie all the way to the aquarium, where they had been able to touch starfish and sea urchins (*Gross*, Greer had whispered as she felt the cold, rough surface of a pink starfish) and watched trained dolphins do tricks in exchange for little silver fish. Hunter had threatened to buy her a T-shirt that said *Gut Salmon?* but she told him she'd rather walk naked down the middle of the street than wear such a thing. "I'd like to see *that*." Hunter had smiled, and she had given him a playful shove that devolved, somehow, into yet another lip-lock.

Not that everything was 100 percent perfect: Hunter may not have been the player Greer thought he was, but he was an incorrigible flirt. He made waitresses blush with his charm and his compliments, and he had the ticket taker at the aquarium panting after him like a dog in heat. But, Greer reasoned, flirting was harmless. As Hunter had told her over and over again, she had no reason to be jealous of anyone. And as she told herself, she'd certainly done her share of flirting in life, so she could hardly blame him too much.

All in all, she felt the way she'd once felt with Brady — that things were working out, that summer was a perfect time for romance, and that she might even love Hunter a little.

No matter what, though, she refused to be all gushy-gooey-gaga over him the way Jessica had been over Connor ever since she got the Lily business sorted out. Greer shuddered a little at the thought. Her cousin and Connor Selden were so disgustingly cute together, so disgustingly *in love*, that they ought to hand out barf bags to anyone in their immediate vicinity.

Her phone beeped then with a text. Speak of the devil — it was Jessica. Greer opened up the picture message. In the photo, Jessica and Connor were each grinning hugely and holding up a giant stuffed-animal version of the iconic Maine lobster.

"Barf," Greer muttered to herself. Naturally, though, she wrote back 2 CUTE U 2!! Her vaguely misanthropic and cynical tendencies aside, she didn't want to be the one to rain on their young-love parade.

She looked at her watch — it was almost time for her lesson. Rather than being her usual five fashionable minutes late, she decided to head out to see Hunter early. Maybe they could get a couple of volleys in before her mother showed up draped in diamonds and a cloud of perfume. Or maybe, she thought, feeling naughty, they could sneak into the locker room for a little pregame private time.

But the court was empty, which surprised her, because Hunter was always early. Had she gotten the time wrong?

She checked her watch again and reassured herself she hadn't. She stood around idly for a while, enjoying the sun on her face and bare arms, until she began to get impatient. Where was he? And where was her mother?

After another few minutes, Greer decided to ask the large, unfriendly woman at the PBAC front desk if Hunter had called in sick. She left her racquet on a bench and walked toward the entrance to the athletic club.

There was a little gazebo on the club's grounds, a quaint cedar structure nearly covered in flowering vines — wild roses, wisteria, and some other flowers Greer couldn't name. She'd seen couples in there, cuddling after their workouts (which, honestly, she'd always found a little gross — wouldn't you want to be *clean* before you snuggled up to someone?). As she passed it, she saw that, as usual, there was a couple in its shady enclave. The woman was leaning over the railing with her back to Greer, and the man was rubbing her back tenderly.

"That feels so good," she heard the woman say. Greer froze. The voice was intimately familiar.

She leaned over and squinted into the gazebo's shade. And who did she see but her mother — being lovingly massaged by *Hunter*.

The anger Greer felt then was so powerful it nearly blinded her. She wasn't surprised at all to see her mother in a compromising position. After all, she'd been flinging herself at men all summer, while Greer had been trying her best to live and let live. But it was one thing when her mother threw herself at a golf pro, and it was another thing entirely when she threw herself at Greer's boyfriend.

And that was leaving aside the issue of Hunter's complicity. She was even madder at him than she was at Cassandra.

"What in the hell is going on here?" she hissed, her fists clenched.

Her mother whirled around, a startled look on her face. "Greer!" she cried. "I was going to meet you on the court!"

"You mean after you got your little love session on?" Greer yelled. She was certain that she'd never been this mad before. She could feel her whole face burning in anger.

"Hey," Hunter interjected, coming toward her. "Calm down."

"Don't you tell me to calm down," Greer hissed. "And get your paws off my mother."

Hunter held up his hands in a gesture of surrender. "She was hurt, Greer," he said quietly. "She hurt her back returning a serve."

Greer turned to her mother, who was looking at her with a deeply wounded expression. "Greer, honey," she said, "it's true. He says I pulled my latissimus dorsi muscle."

As she saw her mother's heavily made-up eyes fill with tears, Greer's certainty that she had caught them in the midst of something deceitful began to crumble.

"You —" she began accusingly, and then stopped.

Her mother stepped gingerly out of the gazebo, clutching her lower back. She didn't seem to be able to stand up straight.

"I'll just go on into the clubhouse," Cassandra whispered. "Maybe you two have something to talk about."

Greer turned back to Hunter, who was staring at her in disbelief. His blue eyes were dark and troubled.

"I thought —" she said.

He shook his head. "No, you *didn't* think. You just jumped to a conclusion because you've never really trusted me." His voice was low and cold. "I really thought things could work out between us, Greer. But now I see that's impossible. Because I refuse to be with someone who automatically assumes the worst about me. I don't need that in my life."

And then he turned and walked away.

Greer watched his retreating back. Mute with sorrow and embarrassment, she felt the prick of tears in the corners of her eyes. She threw the tennis ball she'd been carrying as far as she could. It hit a distant tree with a loud *thwack.*

"With an arm like that, cutie, you should be

playing baseball, not tennis," remarked a guy in a PBAC sweatshirt.

Greer glared at him. If she'd had another ball, she would have thrown it right at his leering face. Instead she gave him the finger, but it didn't make her feel any better.

21

"What do you think, gold or blue?" Lara asked, holding up two silky ruffled tanks. She was having the worst time getting ready for the big barbecue that Connor's family held every August. She'd ripped the dress she'd planned on wearing and spilled Coke on her second-choice skirt, so not being able to decide between the two tops was the least of her worries. (*And indecision seems to be a problem of yours lately*, piped a little voice in her head. *Who will it be, Marco or Drew? Gold or blue?*)

"Blue," Jessica answered.

"Gold," Greer said without looking up from her magazine.

Lara rolled her eyes. "Greer," she admonished, "you can't give advice if you're not even looking."

Greer flipped a page and affixed a little Yes! sticker next to a gauzy beaded gown. "Oh, but I can," she replied. "My fashion sense is so impeccable I can just *feel* that the gold is better."

"Oh, please!" Jessica squealed, nudging Greer with her toe.

Greer rolled over onto her back, languid as a cat. "Seriously, though. Blue tank and blue eyes equals boring. Gold tank and blue eyes equals wow. It's obvious." She propped her long legs against the pearl-colored wall and tucked her hands behind her head.

Lara allowed herself to be convinced by Greer's reasoning, since she'd never seen Greer look bad, not even at six A.M. (perhaps this was because Greer slept in designer pajamas and kept a lip gloss right near her bed so she could swipe it on before she even sat up).

Lara wriggled into the gold top and gave herself a once-over in the mirror. *Not bad*, she thought. *Now if Greer could only tell me what boy to choose . . .*

Lara couldn't help it — she wished that Jessica would just vanish and leave her alone with Greer. Because she *certainly* couldn't talk about Marco with Drew's sister around.

"What are you wearing, Greer?" Jessica asked as she fastened a gold charm necklace around her neck.

"I'm not going," Greer answered.

Lara shot her a confused glance, to which Greer responded, "I don't want to see Hunter." Then Greer filled both her cousins in on what had happened in the gazebo.

Before Lara or Jessica could respond, Greer went on. "And," she said, "I don't want to be at a party with my mother, either, because she still won't forgive me for accusing her of trying to seduce him. She's been giving me the stink-eye for, like, two weeks."

Lara was about to suggest that Greer should consider apologizing, but then she bit her tongue. She didn't think Greer would take kindly to her interference. And for that matter, Lara wasn't sure Cassandra Hallsey was the kiss-and-make-up type. She looked like the kind of woman who could really hold a grudge, even against her own daughter.

"You're crazy not to go," Jessica said as she rubbed a little volumizer into her roots. "Connor's family is so great. Even Liam seems nicer this year. And their new deck is amazing. Connor and I had the best time just watching the seals the other day. He is so cute! He kept going to get me snacks and drinks and he even gave me this amazing foot rub and . . ."

Jessica gushed on, but Lara stopped listening, and from the look of it, Greer did, too. After all, it was highly annoying to listen to someone prattle on about how great their guy was when your own love life was in a shambles. Lara wondered who had it worse: Greer, who currently had no boyfriend, or herself, who was desperately trying to juggle two?

Lara touched up her pedicure (her toenails were now a bright orange), all the while thinking about Drew and Marco. The only good thing she could come up with about her dilemma was that at least Marco wouldn't be at Connor's family's barbecue. He said he was planning on doing some work on his boat.

Jessica felt a light tapping on her forearm.

"Hello? Planet earth to space cadet Lara?" Jessica said. "I was asking you about my brother. How's it going with you guys?"

"Oh, it's great," Lara said breezily, keeping her eyes focused on her toes. "Totally great."

"Come on," Jessica squealed. "I need more info than that! I just told you all about Connor and me!"

Not that we wanted to hear it, Lara thought. She shrugged. "I don't know; it's just really nice."

Jessica sighed dramatically. "God, it's like pulling teeth around here! I'm asking simple questions, you know."

Lara glanced over at Greer, who gave her a sympathetic look in return.

Unfortunately, Jessica saw the look, too. "What's up, you guys?" she demanded. "Why are you staring at each other like that?" Jessica glanced from one cousin to the other, looking hurt. "Do you have secrets or something? Because that's not fair. We're family, and we have to be honest with one another."

Lara felt her stomach tighten. Neither she nor Greer said anything. Greer began to hum under her breath, and Lara became very absorbed in inspecting her toenails again.

Jessica tossed her hair back and shook her finger at them. "You have to include me in your boy talk, Lara, even if the boy you need to talk about is my brother. I mean, come on, how bad can it be? Drew is only, like, the best guy in the world. After Connor, that is."

Lara couldn't help it — she snapped. "Sometimes people just don't feel like blabbing on and on about their *amazing* relationships," she cried, flinging a scarf she had been thinking about wearing to the ground.

Jessica turned pale and dropped the lip gloss she'd been preparing to apply. Lara glared at her for another second and then her anger melted and she began to feel terrible for her outburst.

"Jess . . . I didn't mean that," she said softly. "I'm sorry."

"Whatever," Jessica snapped. Her face was now dark pink. Quickly, she grabbed her bag and turned and walked out of the room.

Greer glanced over to Lara sympathetically. "Sucks," she said. "But at least Jessica doesn't know about your hot Chilean."

Lara nodded glumly. She supposed things could always be worse.

Jessica dug her hand into a big bowl of chips and stuffed far too many of them into her mouth at once. She could be — as her mother's self-help books had informed her — an "emotional eater" (apparently this explained the time she got in a fight with her best friend and subsequently ate half of a chocolate sheet cake in one sitting). So it was a good thing she was a dedicated athlete and burned off most of the calories she consumed. *Otherwise*, she thought, munching on another handful, *I'd be as big as a house.*

She was still feeling upset and confused after Lara's outburst. It was one thing to be snapped at by Greer, but by Lara? Lara was the sweet one, the supportive one, the one who put her arm around you when you were feeling down and gave you a big squeeze. Jessica had been so taken aback by Lara's aggression that she hadn't known how to respond at all. And Lara's apology, though probably sincere, hadn't made her feel any better.

As she mulled all this over, Jessica stood at a short distance from the thick of the Seldens' party, fingering her charm necklace, watching adults and kids alike drinking lemonade and devouring lobster rolls.

She just couldn't figure out what the big deal was. So she'd wanted Lara to share a little about her relationship — was that a crime? Lara knew she was over the whole you're-dating-my-brother grossness, didn't she?

Jessica waved away a fat bumblebee that seemed intent on drowning itself in her lemonade and then sat down on a cedar bench. She watched her parents, tan and glowing with health, chatting with the Seldens and the other guests. Her mother wore a big straw hat and her father sported his fisherman's cap (not that he ever fished — he just went out on the boats and read the newspaper). They were holding hands and smiling.

Jessica's mood shifted quite suddenly and surprisingly, and she felt almost teary with gratitude to see them like that. She realized that she was incredibly lucky to have parents who still loved each other. While Greer's parents had affairs and got divorced, and Lara's mom married and remarried, Jessica's parents had stuck together, and she knew this was not something she should take for granted.

She spied Connor then, coming up from the beach with a bucketful of seashells. He gave the bucket to a bunch of little kids who were building a lopsided mud-rock-seashell fortress in one corner of the deck. She watched as he helped a little boy make a flag for the fortress out of a stick and a cocktail napkin, and she knew she shouldn't take Connor for granted, either.

She helped herself to a couple more chips and then, when Connor disappeared into his house, she sent Greer a quick text. U R MISSING OUT – COME 2 PARTY. She knew Greer wouldn't, but Jessica wanted her to know that the party was fun. Probably the only way she could get Greer out of the house would be to send her a message that said HUNTER = NO SHOW. But she couldn't do that, because she actually saw him over by the grill talking to Liam Selden. (Hunter was even cuter than Connor's brother, which was really saying something.)

Jessica got up and slipped into the house, passing through the living room with its wide-planked floors and big bay windows. In the kitchen, the Seldens were now refilling the lemonade pitchers, a few kids were pawing through the freezer looking for ice cream treats, and half a dozen adults were lingering, making idle chatter.

She smiled at a red-haired woman wearing a violet dress and peered past a large man helping himself to cheese and crackers. She saw the back of Connor's head and decided to sneak up on him. As she tiptoed nearer, she heard him say, "I promise, it's going to be okay."

She craned her neck to see who he was talking to, and she was not at all pleased to see that it was Lily.

Lily was shaking her head and looking uncertain, and then Connor reached out and took her hand.

Oh, no, he didn't.

Jessica halted in her tracks — *what* in the world was her boyfriend doing, holding another girl's hand in the middle of his parents' party? An image of all the lovey-dovey posts Lily had written on Connor's Facebook page flashed into Jessica's head, and she gritted her teeth. This was insane. She was *not* going to put up with Lily trying to steal Connor away from her. And she was going to let Connor know that she was *not* a moron, not some naïve girl who could be jerked around.

Trembling, Jessica started walking toward them — she was going to give those two a piece of her mind — when she heard Connor's voice again, low and urgent. "I told you," he said firmly, "I'm going to help you take care of the baby."

Baby?

Baby?

Jessica's heart seemed to stop, and then plummet down into her espadrilles. She froze for a second, and it felt as if all the blood drained out of her face. Then she took a deep breath, and the blood came rushing back to her cheeks, and her heart started beating hard and fast. And before she even knew what she was doing, she heard herself scream, "Connor Selden, you got Lily *pregnant*?"

A hush fell over the room. Lily's mouth fell open in horror. Behind Jessica, she heard a woman gasp, and when she turned around she saw the redheaded woman steady herself against the counter, looking like she was going to faint. The man she was with put his arm around her to steady her, but he, too, looked like he was about to pass out.

Lily's parents, Jessica thought, suddenly seeing the family resemblance. *They didn't know!*

Lily stifled a sob and then fled from the room. And everyone stared after her — everyone except Connor, that was, who was glaring at Jessica fiercely.

"I can't believe you just did that," he hissed. And then he, too, turned and hurried out of the room, following Lily.

Jessica began to shake uncontrollably. Lily's mother was crying, and Mrs. Selden was fluttering around, trying to offer her tea, a cookie, a tissue — anything to make her feel better. But Lily's mother waved it all away inconsolably.

"What does pregnant mean?" asked one of the kids who'd been reaching into the freezer. He looked to be about three.

This prompted Lily's mother to nearly wail with grief.

Jessica wished that a hole would open up in the floor

and she could fall through it and disappear. Seeing the havoc all around her, she felt more horrible than she'd ever felt. She'd lost Connor to another girl, and now he was going to be a *father*. She felt like her mind might explode from the shock.

As she heard Lily's mother gasping for breath, Jessica understood that she probably wasn't the only one wishing for a hole to disappear into. She couldn't believe she'd outed Lily to her parents. She never, ever wanted to be the bearer of bad news like that. And she wouldn't wish an unwanted pregnancy on anyone, not even her worst enemy. Not even, she thought grimly, on a horrible, evil boyfriend-stealer like Lily Fitzgerald.

23

Lara knew Greer had been right about the gold tank top when she walked out onto the Seldens' deck and saw Drew's face light up. He grinned at her, his green eyes crinkling up at the corners the way they did when he was happy. He motioned for her to come join him at his table.

She threaded her way through the other guests — gingerly, because her heels were extra, extra high — and then sat down next to him. Without saying anything, he offered her a bowl of blueberries. She reached in and took a few; they were tiny and delicious, unlike any blueberries she'd tasted before.

He watched her enjoying them. "I picked them today, just for you."

Lara smiled at this. "How sweet! Was it difficult, harvesting them? Was the bucket heavy? Did your fingers get tired, plucking the blueberries off the bushes?" she teased.

Drew sat up straight in mock indignation. "I'll have you know I got sunburned picking those. *And* I got stung by a bee. But no effort is too much for my Lara."

She giggled and ate some more, which seemed to please him. "Yum."

"Those are wild Maine blueberries, you know," Drew added. "They're the best in the world."

"They taste . . . well, they taste like summer," she told him.

"Exactly," he said. "And, as you may know, they're rich in antioxidants."

Lara decided to tease him a little more because she felt pretty sure she could get away with it. "Did you read that in *Self* magazine or something?"

"No," Drew said, pretending to be very serious. "I read it in *Cosmo*."

Clare Tuttle passed by and grinned at them. "Try the lobster rolls, dears," she called over her shoulder. "They're absolutely fabulous. I think I might have to divorce your father, Drew, and marry Connor's mother, just so I can eat them for the rest of my life."

They grinned at each other — Drew's mother was obsessed with lobster, which was one of the reasons she insisted on coming to Maine each summer — and Lara felt a return of the spark she used to feel every time she and Drew were together.

They'd laughed and teased each other every day at Ahoy, and sometimes when they refilled their coffee carafes at the big machine behind the cash register, their hands would inadvertently touch, and a ripple of desire would begin at that point of contact and spread through her whole body like an electric charge. And though she'd resented the secrecy they'd needed to maintain, she'd also found it exhilarating.

She thought back to the night last summer when they'd gone to see a double feature at the local theater. Though they'd both wanted to see *Dark Knight* and *Iron Man* (Drew, especially, had a soft spot for big summer blockbusters, the cheesier, the better), they hadn't ended up watching a single second of the movies, because they'd been kissing the whole time.

Lara took another handful of blueberries. "Aren't you going to have any?"

Drew shook his head. "They're all for you."

It was just like him to say something like that, Lara thought. He was so generous and so thoughtful — how had she forgotten that about him? Not to mention he was funny and handsome and goofy and loyal.

She took a deep breath. She knew she was about to

make a decision — a decision about Marco, a decision about her relationship with Drew — but she didn't quite know what that decision was yet. She had an idea, though. "I've been thinking," she began.

Drew held up a hand to stop her. "Don't say anything," he interrupted gently. "There's stuff I want to tell you first." His voice was low and warm. It sounded the way it had when they lay in his bed in Ithaca, when she'd snuggled next to him under a down comforter as the snow had fallen softly outside his window, and she'd felt safer than she'd ever felt before.

Drew leaned closer and went on. "I know that it's been a little weird between us lately. I mean, sometimes I get the feeling you're avoiding me because you don't want to deal with telling people about us. And I just want you to know that I understand. I shouldn't have pressured you about it." He smiled ruefully. "I shouldn't have just stopped calling you like that over the summer. I think I got freaked out by everything. And I know I shouldn't have quit the camp job and showed up without warning you. I guess I just wanted to see you so badly . . ."

Lara felt nearly sick with guilt.

He watched her roll a blueberry around in her palm (she'd suddenly lost her appetite) and then continued. "I guess I just want to say that I care about you so much, Lara, and I want us to be whatever and however you want us to be. If you still want to keep everything a secret, I'm cool with that. If you want to tell people, I'm cool with that, too. It's so lame, I know, but it's like there's no such thing as other people to me right now. I'm only interested in you, and what you want."

Startled by his forthrightness, Lara was at a loss for words. He wasn't usually so, well, communicative. All those months they spent apart, he would *never* talk about his feelings, not even when she begged him.

She reached over and touched his hand (but surreptitiously, so that their parents wouldn't see). She felt choked up. "Drew . . . that's not lame. At all. Thank you. And I —"

"Sweetie!" A familiar voice interrupted their tête-à-tête, and Lara's mother came swooping down on them with a giant plate of picnic fare. "Lara-Bear, have you tried these lobster rolls Clare is going on and on about? I kid you not, they are The. Best. Thing. I. Have. Ever. Eaten."

Though Lonnie's appearance came at an awkward moment (and it was *truly* unfortunate that she'd used Lara's childhood nickname in public like that), Lara smiled at her. Her mother sounded as giddy as a teenager. Behind her, Mike Tuttle was trying to balance their cocktails as well as his own heaping plate of food. His shirt said SCRAM TOURISTS, YOU'RE SCARING AWAY ALL THE LAHHBSTAH. Of course, he himself was a tourist, but Lara didn't feel the need to point that out. Perhaps he was wearing it with a sense of irony.

"Honey," Mike said, "you've got mayonnaise on the back of your dress somehow."

Lonnie twirled around, revealing a large oily splotch between her shoulder blades. "However did that happen?" she exclaimed.

Lara rolled her eyes good-naturedly. "You might not know this, but my mom is one of those people who can't eat anything without wearing some of it," she informed Drew. "She's like a toddler that way."

Lonnie sniffed indignantly. "Well, darling, you have a piece of blueberry skin stuck to your front tooth," she said, and then scampered away to eat the rest of her dinner.

Lara reached up and covered her mouth. "Is that true?" she asked through her hand.

Drew smiled. "Um, maybe."

She fished the errant bit of fruit off her tooth with her tongue. "Why didn't you tell me?" she demanded.

"Well," Drew admitted, "it sort of made me feel more comfortable. Like, you looked so beautiful that it was actually making me shy. So when you got that blue front tooth, it kind of made you more . . . approachable."

Lara reached out and swatted his shoulder. "You idiot," she laughed. "I'm always approachable. And you've *approached* me plenty of times, if you know what I mean."

Her voice was full of sexual innuendo, which Drew clearly understood.

"Yeah," he said, grinning. "And I want to *approach* you again, as soon as possible." Under the table, his hand reached out and caressed her knee, then slid a few inches up her thigh.

Lara felt goose bumps rise on her skin and her breath came light and fast. She wanted to be alone with him — she wanted to fall onto a bed with him in a tangle of limbs and hungry mouths. Yes, she knew what she wanted now, and what she wanted was Drew. She wanted to share their secret love with everyone. But there was something she needed to do first.

The sun was setting as Lara approached the bobbing white shape of Marco's boat. She stood uncertainly on the dock as Marco, unaware of her presence, polished the shining oak of the helm. After a moment, she cleared her throat.

Marco turned around, startled. "Oh," he said happily, "it's you!"

Lara looked down at the dock, at her high, uncomfortable sandals. This wasn't going to be easy, so she might as well get it over with as quickly as she could.

"I came here to tell you something," she said. Marco raised his eyebrows expectantly, and she summoned her courage and barreled on. "I think you're really great and

I've loved hanging out with you. You're funny and smart and you're a great sailor and a wonderful big brother to Marcela and I admire you so much."

Marco frowned. "I think I know where this is going," he said, tossing the rag he'd been using to the floor of the boat. He looked down at his feet and his shoulders slumped. He seemed to shrink two inches in height.

Lara nodded sadly. "I'm sorry," she whispered. She fingered her crystal necklace from Drew nervously. "I can't see you anymore."

Marco nodded and Lara just stood there, not knowing what else to say. She felt a little better than she had before she'd made her decision — but she still felt pretty terrible.

"Wow," Marco breathed. "I don't know what to say."

Then a cold but familiar voice broke the silence between them. "That's really *too bad*."

Lara whirled around, her heart pounding. Drew stood behind her, his face as dark as a thunderstorm over the Atlantic.

"I can't believe you did this to me," he said, his eyes blazing. "To us."

Lara was speechless with shock. Drew stared at her for another interminable minute, and then, without saying another word, he turned and stalked back to shore.

Lara held out her hands to Marco, who by now was looking just as furious.

"So you were with him all along, too?" he asked, shaking his head bitterly. "*Wow*. Can I say that again? I know some girls like to get around — you know, like they say, a guy in every port — but I wouldn't have thought *you'd* be that kind of girl."

"I'm not," Lara cried. "Marco, I'm not!"

But she knew the evidence was against her.

Marco bent down and began to polish the helm again with angry energy.

"Marco?" she asked querulously. "Really, you have to understand —"

"I think we're done here," he responded without looking at her at all. "See you around, Lara."

And there was nothing for her to do but walk away, as her tears blurred the shapes of the sailboats and the white wings of the hovering seagulls.

"I just can't even believe it," Jessica moaned. "It's like some after-school special gone horribly wrong."

She lay on Greer's bed, on the impossibly soft, 600-thread-count Egyptian cotton sheets Greer had brought with her from New York, and stared up at the ceiling in misery. The fan whirred, blowing cool air on her hot cheeks. She had stopped sobbing, but her body was still wracked by the occasional teary hiccup.

Greer handed her a cool washcloth, which she took gratefully and placed on her forehead like her mom used to do when she had a fever. "I just can't believe it," Jessica said again. "He told me he loved me, and then he went and got another girl *pregnant*. I mean, it's completely insane."

Greer made an unintelligible answering murmur. Playing therapist was not Greer's strong suit; Jessica realized that. But she was desperate to talk, desperate to have someone explain to her how everything had gone so wrong when it had started out so right. And then the lyrics to that Ziggy Marley song that Mike Tuttle always played popped into her mind without warning: *Some people got the wrong right, some people got the right wrong* . . . She shook her head to banish the melody. What was it about the human brain that made it recall stupid things in times of crisis? She supposed it was a defense mechanism of some sort, but it was annoying. She didn't want to be distracted. Because even though the memory of the events at the barbecue hurt, she wanted to keep going over the scene: Connor's betrayal, her own response, Lily's freak-out.

Jessica couldn't wrap her mind around it, no matter how hard she tried. Connor — the cute, sweet, and wonderful guy she was supposed to lose her virginity to — was more of a player than Greer's Hunter Brown. And even worse, he was going to be a dad.

With that, the tears came again and she didn't bother to wipe them away. She could feel her mascara running down her face, but she didn't care at all.

Greer reached out and patted Jessica's knee. "It's going to be okay," she offered. "I mean, not right away, but eventually it will."

Jessica sniffled and said nothing. She stared at the ceiling fan as it circled around and around and felt the tears trickling down into her ears, and then she rolled over onto her side and stared out the window to the blue-green water a few hundred yards away. Suddenly she wished she were back home in Ithaca, in her warm and cluttered bedroom, instead of this clean, white room with its ivory-colored aromatherapy candles and its spare, modern furniture.

She kicked at the jacquard comforter in sudden anger. "I hate this place," she cried.

"It's going to be okay, I promise," Greer repeated, getting up and fetching Jessica a glass of water from the bathroom. "Here."

Jessica waved the water away. "Just dump it on that damn rug," she said. "Or pour it onto that stupid ottoman over there. What's an ottoman doing in this room, anyway? There's no chair that goes with it. Who designed this stupid place?"

"Someone with a minimalist's sense of decor," Greer said quietly. "I think it's classic, actually."

Jessica was about to launch into a tirade against minimalism, whatever that was, when she heard the door open and the sound of a purse being flung to the floor.

"*Damn* it." Lara's voice sounded weird and strained.

Jessica leaned her head back over the edge of the bed — which made her nose feel even more stuffed up — and saw, upside down, the figure of her stepcousin. Mascara was running down her cheeks, too, and Jessica realized why her voice had sounded so strange: It, too, was thick with tears.

"Oh, no," Greer exclaimed, getting up. "What happened?"

Lara wiped her eyes angrily. "I need to talk to you, Greer," she said. Then she looked at Jessica, completely ignoring the younger girl's obvious distress. "I need to talk to you alone," she clarified.

At that, Jessica sat up, indignation momentarily banishing her sorrow. "What do you mean, alone? What is it that I can't hear?"

Lara shot Greer a look; Greer shrugged.

"Hey," Jessica nearly shouted. "I can see the *significant looks* you guys are sharing over there. I'm not blind." She put her hands on her hips and stood her full five feet eight inches. "And you know what I think? I think that whatever you have to say to Greer, Lara, you can say to me, too."

Jessica tried to seem fierce, but the fact was that she'd never stood up to her cousins like this, and she was a little bit scared about how they would react.

Lara turned to her, her blue eyes blazing. "I don't have to tell you everything, Jessica," she responded, taking off her sweater and throwing it onto the floor. "And if I did tell you, you'd only get more upset. And I just don't feel like dealing with it right now, okay?" A big tear slid down her cheek and landed on the front of her pretty gold tank top.

Seeing that, Jessica softened. She didn't want Lara to feel bad — one of them drowning in misery was more than enough. "Try me," she said. Her voice was gentle.

Greer and Lara exchanged another one of their looks, and Jessica tried not to be annoyed. In the quiet room, the air seemed to crackle with tension.

Lara kicked off her high-heeled sandals and sank onto the lower bunk bed with a heavy sigh. "Fine," she said. "You really want to know?"

Jessica nodded.

Lara bit her lip, then spoke quickly, the words tumbling over one another. "I tried to end things with Marco and Drew overheard and now I've lost both of them."

"Oh, no," Greer whispered.

But Jessica could only stare. *Marco?* Who the hell was Marco? Had Lara been seeing another guy this summer? But what about Drew? She opened her mouth, but nothing came out. Her poor brother! He'd quit his job and come to Pebble Beach just to be with Lara, and she'd repaid him by *cheating*?

She realized that she was heading toward the door, and she watched her hand as it reached out and turned the knob. She couldn't be in the room anymore, not with those two. She'd had enough betrayals for the evening. In fact, she'd had enough betrayals to last for the rest of her life. First Connor and Lily, then Lara running around on Drew. And Lara not telling her, and Greer knowing and not telling her — it was all so awful she couldn't stand it.

"Jess, where are you going?" Greer's voice was uncharacteristically soft and pleading.

Jessica whirled around, her blonde ponytail whipping against the doorframe. "Away," she hissed. "So you two can keep having your horrible secrets. I don't want to hear any more of them."

"Jessica, please wait," Lara called.

But Jessica didn't hear her, because she was already out the door.

25

Greer yawned and stretched, wriggling her toes under the blankets in sleepy pleasure. She'd just had the best dream: She and Hunter had sailed out to one of the tiny rocky islands that dotted the water beyond Pebble Beach, and then they'd strolled along the shore as the salty waves splashed their feet. Then, out of nowhere, a beautiful red bird had appeared in front of them, and the bird told them that it was going to start growing very quickly, and that when it got big enough, it would take them across the ocean to a different island where they would be given a castle to live in.

Greer snuggled deeper into the covers and tried closing her eyes again so she could pick up where the dream had left off. But she was startled by a crash from down in the kitchen — likely Uncle Carr, attempting to wield the giant cast iron skillet to make scrambled eggs — which meant that, like it or not, she was awake for good.

As the spell of the dream lifted, Greer's mood sank. She wasn't going to be able to live on a beautiful island with a Hunter and a giant red bird because Hunter wasn't speaking to her. Jessica, who was not as desirable a dream companion but who was nevertheless one of Greer's favorite people, was also not speaking to her. And, to top it all off, Greer's own mother had been avoiding her for weeks now.

Everything sucked.

Greer swung her long legs over the bed and tucked her feet into her pink silk slippers. The room was empty; as usual, she'd slept later than both of her cousins. As she stepped into the bathroom to begin her morning routine (face washed with Dr. Hauschka Rose Facial Scrub, toned with L'Oréal HydraFresh Toner, and moisturized with La Prairie Skin Caviar Luxe Cream), Greer thought about Cassandra. The weird thing was, before the whole Hunter blowup, her mom had been nicer to her than she ever had been before. When her parents were together, it seemed like Cassandra could hardly make time for Greer in between her appointments at Frederic Fekkai, her shopping sprees at Barneys and Bergdorf's, and her lunches with other rich and idle women. But when they got to Pebble Beach, suddenly Cassandra wanted to eat breakfast with Greer, and take walks with her, and tennis lessons, and long drives through the Maine countryside. *When she wasn't throwing herself at men, of course*, Greer thought.

Still, it made Greer feel like the worst daughter ever. Her mother had finally decided to pay some attention to her and she'd repaid her by accusing her of fooling around with an 18-year-old boy. Greer scrubbed her face vigorously, as if this would help her wipe away her bad behavior as well as any dead skin cells.

The water she splashed on her cheeks was bracingly chilly. She buried her face in a soft blue towel, and then peeked over the top of it to meet her hazel gaze in the mirror.

"Greer Hallsey," she whispered, "you are going to apologize to your mother."

That was what her father used to say, and Greer had always resented it. But this time, she knew that it was what she needed to do.

She finished the rest of her grooming routine and then she pulled on a pair of wide-legged shorts and a fitted green top. She made the uncharacteristic decision to leave the room without makeup — not that she'd ever leave the *house* that way, of course, but she didn't think it was necessary to have a layer of foundation and a dozen other products on her face while she went to talk to her mother.

As she padded down the hallway, she heard another loud crash from the kitchen, followed by a softer expletive. Yes, it was Uncle Carr, making his breakfast. He made amazing scrambled eggs — they made the ones at Balthazar seem about as flavorful as yellow packing peanuts — but still, Greer couldn't understand why he insisted on using a pan so heavy he seemed to drop it every time he tried to pick it up.

Not that that was her problem, of course. Her problem was much more complicated. But she aimed to make it better, starting with Cassandra Hallsey.

As she climbed the stairs to the house's top story, she saw a large ficus tree positioned outside her mother's door like a sentry. Brushing past its shiny leaves, she knocked gently.

"Clare, is that you?" Cassandra Hallsey called. "Because I already told you, I don't want to go to that flea market you're so fascinated by. I went to a flea market once when I was a kid, in New Jersey, and that was more than enough for me. People setting up tables to try to sell their trash to other people? I just don't get it. Now, if you were offering to take me to a Neiman Marcus, say, I could probably find something I wanted."

Greer felt a little smile tremble on her lips. Her mother

was . . . Well, she just was who she was. She pushed open the door. "Mom?" she whispered.

Cassandra was curled up in a deep armchair underneath one of the skylights. The rays of the sun slanted down on her coppery hair, making it glow, but Greer could see that there were dark shadows under her eyes.

"Oh, it's you," her mother said, her tone unreadable.

Greer watched as her mother rose and walked over to the dresser, where she pulled out a sweater and tied it around her shoulders. Cassandra was wearing an outfit the likes of which Greer had never seen on her before: heavy cotton yoga pants, a high-necked, long-sleeved, blue T-shirt, and what looked like a pair of orthopedic sandals. With *socks.*

"Oh, my God," Greer said. "What —" She was going to say, *"What happened to you?"* but she realized that might not sound very nice. She cleared her throat and began again. "You look, um, comfortable," she offered.

Cassandra gave her a mirthless smile but said nothing. She returned to her chair and folded her legs underneath her. Beside her on the table was the latest issue of *Town & Country* and a copy of a book called *WTF?: Speaking the Foreign Language of Your Teenage Children.*

Greer pointed to the volume, which had a lurid pink cover. "Does it tell you that 'sick' means awesome? Or that 'crib' means house?" she asked lightheartedly.

Cassandra gave her a long look. "It says that in teenagers, the frontal lobes of the brain are undergoing a process of maturation, which renders them essentially useless until they get a little bit older. The frontal lobes, in case you didn't know, are the brain parts that help you control your impulses and make good judgments. In other words, they're what makes you a good, kind person." She stopped and raised her eyebrows at Greer expectantly.

Wow, Greer thought. *Mom sounds like my shrink.* She sat down on the bed across from her mother and folded her hands together. "I guess my frontal lobes are still under construction," she admitted. Cassandra nodded slightly, and Greer took a deep breath and went on. "If I'd stopped to think about it — which I didn't — I would have known that you'd never hit on Hunter. I never should have accused you like that, and I'm sorry. I wish I could take it back." *Because I hurt you*, Greer thought, *but also because I hurt Hunter. And I can't just walk into his bedroom and apologize.*

Her mother took a sip of her coffee and then set the cup back into its saucer with a clink. "I appreciate your apology," she said softly.

"Actually I'm not done," Greer told her. "I want to apologize for being sort of hard on you all summer. I mean, I know you were just trying to have a nice time out here. And I should have been better about letting you do that."

A faint smile began to dance across her mother's lips. "Well, you *did* have a point when you told me that I shouldn't wear your miniskirts. I mean, let's face it, I'm a far cry from eighteen." Cassandra paused. "But more seriously, Greer, I realize that I was not on my best behavior this summer, either. I shouldn't have been so . . . *flirtatious*. For instance, I should have done a better job of covering up these." Here she pointed to her chest and smiled. "I mean, I don't have to act like a total man-eater, right? I can be a little more subtle? Just because your father turned into a middle-aged man-slut doesn't mean I have to act in a similar fashion."

Greer grinned. She was so grateful that her mother was going to forgive her (and so grateful that she seemed intent on acting her age from now on) that she very nearly leapt across the room and crawled into Cassandra's lap. Instead, though, she pulled a blank piece of paper from a pad on a nearby table and began to quickly sketch something. She wasn't an amazing artist, but she was good enough to illustrate the idea that had just occurred to her. "Check this out," she said, smiling. "You're going to love it."

Her tongue between her lips in concentration, she

drew a woman wearing a formfitting tank top and a short (but not *too* short!) matching tennis skirt. On the shirt Greer wrote the team name she'd just decided on — The Cougars — in big script. Pleased with her work, she handed the paper to her mother. "It's our uniforms for the tournament next week," she said eagerly. "They'll be all pink, with glittery lettering. We'll match. What do you think?"

Cassandra squealed with delight. "Greer, I love it!" she cried. "It's fantastic!" She clutched the piece of paper excitedly. "And I know just the place we can get these made. The lady who owns the little dress shop on Beach Street used to work with Donna Karan." Cassandra looked as if she was going to start talking fashion, but then she stopped and smiled gently at her daughter. "Oh, Greer," she said, her voice softer now. "I'm so glad you want to be on my team. And I mean in life, not just in tennis."

Greer felt a lump rising in her throat, and she nodded. "I love you, Mom," she said. Then she stood up and gave Cassandra a high five. "Now, I hope you're ready to kick some mother-daughter ass next Saturday!"

The morning of the tennis tournament dawned warm and bright. By nine A.M. the stands at the Pebble Beach Athletic Club were full of dads and little kids ready to cheer on the moms and older daughters who had signed up to play. There were clusters of balloons, a lemonade stand, and a table displaying the trophies for first, second, and third place.

To Greer, who had never attended an event so authentically *wholesome*, it was a foreign but exciting scene. She eyed the snow cone machine hungrily, and promised herself that she'd get a cherry snow cone right after her warm-up. As she and her mother stretched their hamstrings and did a few jumping jacks, she felt the tension she'd been carrying in her shoulders melt away.

On their way to the PBAC, Greer had asked her mother to stop at Hunter's house. She'd jumped out of the car, dashed up his front steps, and slipped a letter under his door.

Dear Hunter,
I know you're angry at me, and I completely understand why. I was acting like a crazy person. I'm so, so sorry. My mother told me it's because my frontal lobes aren't fully developed yet, but I think that it's probably because I'm just an idiot. A jealous, suspicious idiot. I'm trying to change that, though, believe me. I know you might not want to see me ever again, but I hope that you can forgive me anyway. I care about you so much, and I wish I had trusted you

from the beginning. Thank you for being a better person than I am.

Love,
Greer

Then she'd run back to join her mother in the convertible, and they'd blasted Taylor Swift on the CD player, singing all the way to the tennis tournament in the matching pink outfits Greer had made for them.

After a virtually sleepless night, Lara had risen with a sense of purpose. She was still feeling sad, but she was resigned to resolve what had happened between her and Drew. She knew he was furious at her, and she didn't expect to change that. But she also knew she had to tell him that she was sorry.

She crept downstairs and lingered outside the dining room, watching Drew (or Drew's back, anyway) as he consumed the giant stack of pancakes that was his favorite breakfast. She felt sort of like a spy, but without the cool spy gadgets, like watches that were actually recording devices or earrings that were video cameras. And instead of wanting to eavesdrop on her quarry, she just needed to go up and talk to him face-to-face.

The trouble was, she was afraid. She couldn't bear the thought of Drew turning away from her again, the way he did when he'd overheard her trying to break things off with Marco. She couldn't bear it if he looked at her with his emerald eyes as dark and cold as the Arctic Ocean.

Her mother came down the hall and swatted Lara lightly on the butt. "What are you doing lurking around like that?" she asked as she breezed by in a cloud of her favorite rose-water scent. "He won't bite, you know,"

Drew, having heard Lonnie's chirpy voice, turned around and spotted Lara in the doorway. His face was expressionless as she walked forward and sat down across from him at the gleaming ebony table.

She reached into the fruit bowl and pulled out a banana, which she began to peel nervously. Her stomach was tied in too many knots for her to actually eat it, so after it had been skinned she set it down on the table. Instead of looking at Drew, she just stared at the poor naked banana. She could feel Drew waiting for her to say something, and the whole house seemed heavy with silence.

"I'm sorry," she whispered.

"What are you apologizing to the banana for?" Drew asked.

Lara looked up at him then, and her heart gave a tiny leap of hope. He'd made a joke, and even if he wasn't smiling, it meant that he couldn't be so mad that he actually *hated* her, which was what she'd been afraid of.

"I was apologizing to you," she told him, her voice gaining strength. "It's just hard to look a person in the eye when you've done what I did. I never meant to hurt you, Drew. I should have told you about Marco, but I was confused, and things just got out of hand." She paused, then corrected herself. It was important to take all the blame that she deserved. "I mean, I *let* things get out of hand. When we stopped talking, and when you didn't show up here, I missed you so much. But instead of calling you or sending you an e-mail, I guess I sort of tried to forget you. I know that doesn't make any sense — I can't understand it myself. All I can say is that I'm so sorry, and I hope that you don't hate me." She looked down at the banana again. "Or if you do hate me, I hope you'll get over it sooner rather than later."

Drew reached across the table and touched her hand. "I could never hate you, Lara," he assured her. "But I am really . . . really hurt."

She nodded meekly. "I know."

He let his finger wander over her knuckles, and then he touched the chipped polish on her thumb. "But I know that I'm to blame, too." He grimaced a little and then went on. "I mean, as I said the other day, when we got in that fight over the phone, it was my own fault that I never called you back. And then not telling you that I was going to be a camp counselor instead of coming to Pebble Beach wasn't cool at all."

Lara shook her head. "It wasn't," she agreed.

He withdrew his hand and leaned back in his chair. "You may have noticed that I'm not the world's best communicator."

Lara's response was good-naturedly sarcastic. "Oh, really? You don't say."

"Really," he confirmed, apparently missing her taunt entirely. "And then just showing up like I did, assuming that everything could be the same, and trying to convince you that we should tell everyone about our relationship — that was sort of uncool, too."

Lara was surprised at how easily he took a share of the blame. She was the one who'd kissed another person, and then lied about it, and yet Drew was doing most of the apologizing. The thought occurred to her that perhaps Drew had a guilty secret of his own. She felt her brows come together in frowning concentration.

"Before you start wondering if I cheated and came back to Pebble Beach because I felt guilty, I didn't," Drew said, reading Lara's mind precisely. "I came back for you."

Immediately, Lara felt like shrinking into her chair. He'd come back for her, and she'd just continued to make out with another guy. What kind of horrible person was she?

211

"And I don't think you're a terrible person or anything like that," he said, and Lara practically fell off her seat. Since when was Drew psychic? "I just think you made a mistake, and I think I made some mistakes, too."

Lara smiled shyly at him. Their conversation was going so much better than she expected. She felt like if it kept going in this vein, she might even be able to eat that banana after all. "So does that mean —"

But Drew held up a hand to cut her off. "I still think that maybe we should be . . . apart for a while." He paused while his words sunk in for them both. He was sad, Lara could tell, and she was, too. But she knew what he said was right. "We live hundreds of miles away from each other," he continued. "And when we were together it was always like playing some kind of secret game. I think that warped things a little."

Lara nodded, but she couldn't quite speak. The truth, after all, wasn't always easy to take. What they'd had had been wonderful, but it belonged to a particular place and time that was neither here nor now. Something had changed between them in these summer months. She knew that she would always have memories of him at Ahoy, on the sunny beach, in the quiet of a bedroom empty but for the two of them — and that would have to be enough.

She felt a single tear make its way down her cheek and land on the shiny lacquered table with an audible plop.

Then Drew stood up and came around to where she was sitting, and he pulled her from her chair and gave her a hug.

"I'll always love you, you know that," he murmured into her hair.

She nodded again, into his chest, and then she managed to find her voice. "I'll always love you, too," she whispered.

They stood that way for what felt like a long time, and then they tenderly kissed. It was their way of saying good-bye.

Lara cried in her room for a while, letting the hurt of losing Drew wash over her. Then she decided it was time to search the house for Jessica. Painful as it was, she had made her peace with Drew, and now it was time to do the same with his sister. *If Jessica will let me, that is*, Lara thought. In talking to Drew, she'd been reminded again about the importance of honesty. If you cared about someone, you didn't hide the truth from them, not even if you thought it would hurt them. You could tell white lies once in a while ("Yeah, I really *do* like that mauve-and-puce-striped sweater of yours!") but nothing more than that. And Marco certainly hadn't been a white lie.

She checked the deck, the living room, the two other rental houses, and the beach, but there was no Jessica. Lara made the whole circuit again, with no luck, and then she returned to the dining room. The banana was still on the table, skinned and defenseless. She picked it up and took a bite, even though she still wasn't the least bit hungry.

Well, in that case, now you better go find Marco, said the voice in her head. At that Lara sighed wearily. There was so much explaining and apologizing to do. Who would have guessed she'd be able to get herself in so much trouble in only three months?

With a heavy heart, she climbed onto one of the house bikes and cycled slowly toward the harbor. White blossoms of Queen Anne's lace lined the road on either side, and here and there, Lara saw the dark glint of ripening blackberries. The day was perfect, but it failed to cheer her up.

When she saw the bright, multicolored sail of Marco's boat, she leaned her bike against a fence and hesitantly approached. Even though she knew that he deserved a real apology, there was a part of her that hoped he wasn't around. *I could send him an e-mail*, she thought. *Maybe that's the best thing to do.* She told herself that she'd walk a few more feet, and if Marco didn't appear, then she'd just turn around and go home.

But then Marco, wearing a white T-shirt that seemed to glow against his dark skin, climbed up the ladder from the hull. The look he gave her was very unwelcoming.

"Lara," he intoned coldly.

She froze in her tracks. "Marco, I came to apologize," she said. "And to explain."

He gazed out over the blue water. "I don't need an explanation."

Lara gathered her courage up. "But I want to give you one." She took a few more steps toward the boat, until she was standing right at the edge of the mooring. "Drew was my boyfriend, but then we basically broke up. He sort of disappeared for a month without talking to me. So when I met you, I considered myself single." She bit her lip and then went on. "And I really liked you. You were hilarious and smart and totally gorgeous . . . I mean, you still *are* those things."

Marco crossed his arms and gave her a dark look. "Fat lot of good it does me."

Lara hung her head and stared down at her feet. "So you and I, we were having this great time," she stated, without looking up to see if he agreed with her. "And then Drew showed up and acted as if we'd never had a fight. And the thing is, I still cared about him. I mean, you can't just forget someone you dated because they don't call you for weeks." She cleared her throat but still kept her eyes on her toes. She could hear Marco moving around on the boat, and she hoped he was still listening. "I just wasn't strong enough to know what I wanted. And in a way, I still don't. All I know is that I hurt both of you, and I *lost* both of you, and

I've never been sorrier about anything in my life." Finally she raised her eyes, which by now were full of tears.

Marco had left the boat and was standing by her on the dock. His expression seemed kinder. As she gazed at him, she thought she saw the glimmer of a sad smile on his face. "Well," he said, "I guess there probably couldn't have been a future for us anyway. I mean, we live almost a thousand miles away from each other. I just wish that you had been honest with me. I wish you'd told me about Drew. I would have hung out with you anyway. I can have girls just as friends, you know."

Lara sighed. Marco was right. "I'm just so sorry," she said.

"Well," Marco replied, reaching out for her hand, "I forgive you. I don't believe in grudges."

Lara looked up at him, smiling gratefully. "So does that mean we can be friends?" she asked, hope in her voice.

Marco didn't reply right away, but when he did, he said that he thought they could. "If we weren't friends, I guess I'd miss your tirades about the evils of mass consumption and the sheeplike mentality of American society." Lara clapped her hands over her ears in dismay, but she could still hear him parroting her lectures about the dreadful influence of advertising and the problem of people purchasing goods in excess of their basic needs.

"You're just trying to punish me," she cried.

At this, Marco began to laugh. "Sorry," he said. "Couldn't help it."

Lara grinned ruefully. "So I guess I'll just have to send you anti-capitalist e-mails," she offered.

"Sounds like a plan," Marco replied.

Marco held out his hand, and Lara shook it.

"Friends," she said.

"Friends," he agreed.

27

The August breeze lifted Jessica's golden bangs from her forehead as she parked her bike outside Lily Fitzgerald's front gate. Roses spilled over the picket fence in brilliant clusters of pink and yellow, and here and there, fuzzy, striped bumblebees dive-bombed into lilies and emerged covered in pollen.

The Fitzgeralds' house was a modest but utterly charming New England beach cottage, complete with weathered cedar-shingle siding, freshly painted white shutters, and blue hydrangea bushes flanking the red front door. There were window boxes full of pansies and a pair of birdbaths, each one being enjoyed by a coterie of small, brown birds.

It looked like a house where nothing bad could ever happen, Jessica thought. But something bad *had* happened, and Jessica had played a role in it. Obviously she wasn't to blame for the fact that Lily was pregnant, but it was definitely her fault that Lily's parents had found out when and how they did.

The whole thing just sucked, plain and simple. But Jessica had decided that part of getting over Connor was letting him go, and wishing him the best in his new life with Lily and their baby. She was still deeply hurt and extremely confused, but she felt sorry for him, too. Who wanted a baby at seventeen? Certainly not Jessica, and she was pretty sure neither Lily nor Connor wanted one, either. At least Connor was taking responsibility for the situation and being a good partner to Lily.

Partner. Ugh, she hated that word. And the little voice inside her head cried out, *He was supposed to be yours! Not hers!* But she gritted her teeth and told the little voice to shut up before it started calling Lily a redheaded slut or something. It was not the time to be mean; it was time to make amends. Because the fact of the matter was, Jessica would be leaving soon, and she'd be going back to school and her regular teenage life of sports and parties and homework, while Connor and Lily would remain in Pebble Beach, catapulted suddenly into adulthood.

Lucky you and Connor never did it, the voice said. *Otherwise that whole teen mom thing could have been you.* She felt a shiver run up her spine.

"Jessica?" came a high, questioning voice.

Jessica glanced up to see Lily standing in the doorway with a confused look on her face. Even though the girl couldn't possibly be showing yet, she was already wearing a soft, shapeless dress. Her hair was done up in two long, red braids, and she reminded Jessica of Pippi Longstocking. A sad, pale, pregnant Pippi Longstocking.

Jessica felt herself flush. "I guess I've been standing out here for a while," she admitted. "Do you have a minute?"

Lily nodded, and Jessica pushed open the gate and walked up the stone pathway to the Fitzgeralds' front stoop. She stopped right in front of Lily and looked her straight in the eye. "I came to apologize," she said firmly. "I never, ever should have yelled the way I did. It was your right to tell your parents what was going on, and I ruined it for you. I'm so sorry. And I also want to say that I hope you and Connor are really happy. I'm sure you'll have a beautiful baby." Jessica felt a knot rising in her throat, and the knot threatened to become a sob, which in turn threatened to blossom into a full-on cry fest. So she quickly turned and started down the walkway to the gate. She'd said what she came to say, and now she could go back home and pull the covers up over her head and feel sorry for herself for the next week.

"Wait," Lily called, and started down the path after her. "Jessica, wait."

"What?" Jessica wheeled around and saw Lily reaching out for her.

"Just hang on," Lily said. "You've got it all wrong. Connor's not the father."

Jessica's mouth fell open. *Connor's not the father?*

"The dad is a guy from my history class," Lily went on, her voice now flat. "Andy Marcus. He's a total wannabe frat guy *jerk*, and I can't believe I was stupid enough to fall for him. He can't even *spell*, Jessica, and I thought I loved him." She shook her head at the memory, or maybe at her own foolishness. "He won't even talk to me now. He says the kid's not his, even though he's the only guy I ever slept with. And so Connor, who has been one of my best friends since we were six, told me that he would help me out however he could." She turned to Jessica and looked her in the eye. "That's it," she said firmly. "He's just being a good friend, because that's the kind of guy he is. He loves you, Jessica, not me."

Jessica hardly knew what to say. There were so many emotions coursing through her — surprise, relief, happiness, pity — that she felt like she might be going temporarily crazy.

"Let's take a walk," Lily said, and Jessica, not knowing what else to do, fell in step beside her. They strolled down the quiet road as tiny white butterflies danced in the wildflowers on either side of them.

Lily reached over to the road's shoulder and plucked a pretty blue flower and tucked it behind her ear. Jessica noticed in that moment how beautiful she was. "I told Connor not to tell anyone," Lily explained softly. "For a long time he was the only person who knew. Until that party, and then suddenly a lot of people knew."

"I'm really sorry about that," Jessica managed to get out. Her mind was filled with thoughts of Connor — she should have known he'd never betray her like that. No wonder he'd been so furious with her. She felt like bursting into tears. For her, for Connor, for Lily.

Lily shrugged. "Well, my parents needed to know sometime," she admitted. "You just sort of speeded up the process."

Jessica smiled ruefully. That was certainly a generous way of looking at it. "Did I ever," she agreed.

They walked a little farther down the road, and in the distance Jessica could see the buildings of downtown Pebble Beach, with their brightly colored storefronts and their cheerful signs.

"This is a nice place to raise a kid," she offered shyly.

Lily nodded. "That's what I tell myself," she said. She put her hands on her belly. "I'm scared, though. I mean, terrified."

Jessica put her arm around Lily's thin shoulders. "I'm sure it's scary," she whispered.

Jessica watched as a single tear slid down Lily's freckled cheek. "This never should have happened," Lily said. "But it did. And so I just have to go on. My parents will help me, too, even though they're still pretty upset."

"You're going to be okay," Jessica said.

Lily wiped the tear away fiercely. "I know. Eventually it will all be fine. In about twenty years." She laughed humorlessly. "But you know what? Despite all of it, I think I love the baby already."

You'd better, Jessica thought grimly. *Because babies are no freaking picnic.* "You'll be a great mom," she assured Lily. "I just know it."

To her surprise, Jessica felt herself reaching out to give Lily a warm hug. Lily hugged her back, and Jessica understood why Connor was such a good friend to Lily. She was a special person.

And so was Connor.

And now she'd pushed him away.

After saying good-bye to Lily, Jessica turned and set off, determined to remedy that.

"Thirty-love," barked the umpire at the Pebble Beach Athletic Club's annual Mother-Daughter Tennis Tournament. The aging amplifiers gave a hiss and a squawk as he cleared his throat. "Serving for the Pebble Beach Princesses is Monica Milner of Greenwich, Connecticut."

Greer wiped the sweat from her brow and stifled the string of curses she felt like uttering. Even after a summer of lessons, she still didn't understand tennis scoring — why did they use the term "love" anyway, instead of simply saying "zero"? And how many games were in a set, and how many sets in a match?

Of course, she didn't need to know the answers to these questions to know that she and her mother were seriously losing to Monica Milner and her daughter, Madeline.

And surprisingly, it wasn't even her mother's fault. Cassandra had begun the summer a poor player: She'd been more interested in flirting with Hunter and making catty remarks about Monica, the woman who wintered in Aspen instead of Gstaad and wore diamonds so blingy she looked like a white, female version of P. Diddy. She'd also had a terrible serve and a short attention span, so that every time Hunter tried to explain the physics of the tennis serve — believing, perhaps mistakenly, that this would help her master it — she'd end up spacing out completely and then asking him who he thought was a better player, Rafael Nadal or Roger Federer. (Cassandra preferred the former because she thought he was cuter.)

But thanks to Hunter's patient and knowledgeable tutelage, Cassandra Hallsey had blossomed into a reasonably decent player. Her serve was more than adequate, and, given the chance to use it, she had a wicked overhead smash.

It was Greer who was screwing everything up, even though she was better at the game. In fact, she was a natural athlete, but (a) she wouldn't admit it, and (b) she hated sports in general and team sports especially.

No matter how hard she tried, Greer couldn't keep her head in the game, because she kept thinking about Hunter. Of course she'd scanned the crowd when she arrived, and she'd peered hopefully into the employees' lounge area, but she hadn't seen him. Which, she admitted to herself, was no surprise. Why would a guy she'd publicly accused of hitting on her mother want to watch her hit a yellow ball back and forth across a net? She could only hope that he'd gotten her letter. And that he'd read it instead of just wadding it up and tossing it into the trash. Though she had to admit, she'd understand if that was what he did.

"Greer," Cassandra hissed. "Snap to it, will you? That wench is going to serve it straight for your head."

Greer gripped her racquet with both hands and crouched down a little, preparing to return the ball. When it came spinning at her, she ran forward, extended her arm, and slammed the ball hard — right into the net.

"Shit," she muttered.

Her mother stalked over to her side. "Greer," she said firmly. "You know I love you. And so I mean what I'm going to say in the most loving possible way. *If you don't help me kick that fishwife's ass, I'm going to hang you upside down by the ankles using my collection of Hermès scarves.*" Then she pinched Greer's cheeks and grinned. "Seriously, honey, pull it together."

The umpire's voice crackled over the speaker. "Forty-love. Game point."

Time for a rally, Greer told herself. *Come on, you can do it.*

She glanced down at the sparkling Cougars name on her shirt and tried to draw inspiration from it. If she couldn't do it for herself, maybe she could do it for her mother, who would rather have her head shaved down to the bare skull than lose to Monica Milner. After all, one could always purchase a very nice wig — but one could not purchase a victory.

Monica's first serve went straight into the net and Greer felt her heart lift with hope. Serve number two came seconds later, and Greer, using all her concentration and power, dove for it.

And missed.

Cassandra Hallsey paced back and forth under the shade of a large maple tree. "Okay, we lost the first set. But it's the best two out of three to win, which means we can still take them down. I can't stand those Princesses. Did you see how that Monica was gloating? I didn't know a face with that much Botox in it could be so expressive."

Greer leaned against the trunk tiredly. Yes, Monica had gloated in a very unsportsmanlike fashion, and Madeline had given Greer the serious stink-eye. But maybe they'd earned the right to rub it in a little. After all, the Cougars hadn't scored a single point in the last game.

Greer rolled her ankles around, warming them up again. "It's my fault," she said, hearing a weird little pop in her ankle as she did so.

Cassandra nodded. "I won't lie to you. It is your fault. But you're a great player, Greer. You can do this! Remember Hunter and what he taught you!"

Greer grimaced. She was remembering Hunter all right, but it had nothing to do with tennis. She was remembering how strong his arms were, and thinking about the knowing softness of his hands. She was daydreaming about how it felt to lie next to him under the stars, feeling the rise and fall of his chest against her cheek and hearing the steady beat beat beat of his heart.

Her mother interrupted her thoughts. "Remember, shot preparation is as important as the actual shot itself. Without good preparation, your body can't get the power and control you need to hit a good shot."

Greer gazed up into the leaves of the maple as her mother droned on and on about topspin and forehand grip and net exchanges and reaction time. Cassandra had never been this passionate about anything before, unless you counted Proenza Schouler's spring collection last year, which she said was "absolute genius and perfection." Who knew a tennis competition could bring out such fervor in a Park Avenue matron?

Maybe, Greer thought, *this tree will fall down on my*

head and kill me and I won't have to play the next game. She sort of hoped that it would.

She was considering making a wish for a lightning strike or a tidal wave — *anything* to stop the tournament from continuing on — when she heard her mother squeal. Greer tore her eyes from the tree branches to see her mother scurrying away, arms outstretched, giddily running to embrace a very familiar-looking figure.

Greer pushed herself off the tree and squinted. It couldn't be. Was it — was that Hunter?

She held her breath and then let it out in one great whoosh that was half relief, half nervousness. It was Hunter, wearing a PBAC baseball cap and his tennis whites, and he was coming toward her with his arm linked through her mother's.

She gave him a small, hopeful smile, and he returned it times ten. His blue eyes were as clear and untroubled as the summer sky.

"You got my letter," she whispered.

He leaned in close to her ear and she could feel his warm breath on her neck. "Yes, but let's talk about that later." And then he stepped back and clapped his hands together briskly. "Ladies!" he exclaimed. "I believe we have a match to win."

He held out his arms to bring them into a huddle. Greer almost shivered when he touched her. She wanted him to touch her *more*. But she shook her head to clear her thoughts. Now was the time to focus on the game.

"Okay," he said confidently. "We're going to go with an up-and-back strategy, because we want to be thinking both offensively and defensively. Greer, I want you to play at the net. Cassandra, you're going to play baseline."

This time, Greer had no problem paying attention to her instructions, and when the Cougars walked onto the court for the next set, there was a spring in Greer's step. She narrowed her eyes at her opponents, the Pebble Beach Princesses, who were looking too confident for their own good. When Greer caught Madeline glaring at her, she brought her hand up to her cheek, slyly raised her middle finger, and smiled.

It was Greer's turn to serve. She bounced the ball at her side, savoring the annoyed look that Madeline was now giving her. Then she threw the ball into the air, slammed it with her racquet, and watched it zing across the net to land inches from the line. It bounced up, and Madeline swung hard.

And missed.

Now, *that* was more like it, Greer thought.

"Fifteen-love," called the umpire, and Greer grinned. She was going to enjoy this game a lot more than the one before it.

Her mother giggled in delight, and Greer prepared for

another serve. The Cougars were going to win — she just knew it.

And when they did, and the Pebble Beach Princesses stormed off the court in a huff, Hunter came running out to where she stood by the net and picked her up and whirled her around. She let her racquet fall to the ground as she wrapped her arms around him. When their mouths met in a passionate kiss, Greer realized that the crowd was applauding wildly.

She wasn't sure if they were clapping because the Cougars won, or because the coach was kissing his star player. But she didn't care at all. She just closed her eyes and lost herself in Hunter's forgiving embrace.

29

As Jessica rode by the pier on her way to Connor's house, the bright clanking of the boats' rigging against their masts filled her ears with what sounded like a chorus of tiny bells. Above her, the white clouds, fat as sheep, drifted lazily on the breeze.

It was an achingly beautiful day — the kind of day that made her never want to leave this little town with its sandy roads, its rocky beaches, and its chilly, blue ocean. She passed by Izzy's Ice Cream and the crepe shop and watched a small boy chase a ball down the sidewalk. It seemed strange to her that a town that looked so peaceful and bucolic could hold so many secrets and so much drama.

A fisherman, his truck loaded down with the morning's catch, drove by and blew her a loud, appreciative kiss.

Or maybe, she reflected wryly, the town was plenty peaceful on its own — it was the Tuttles who brought the drama.

She could only hope that a visit to Connor's house would settle the next bit of unpleasant business of which she was a part. Lily had forgiven her, and she hoped Connor would, too. (And she hoped that she'd be feeling a little more forgiving toward Lara eventually as well.)

She pedaled faster and tiny pearls of sweat broke out on her forehead. She was glad she'd opted for her traditional summer outfit of a tank and shorts rather than following Greer's constant advice to dress "more like a sixteen-year-old girl, and less like a six-year-old boy."

She tried to decide if she was mad at Greer, too, and she came to the conclusion that yes, she was. But Jessica was by nature a forgiving person — having two older brothers who spent their entire childhoods teasing and harassing her had taught her a lot about letting bygones be bygones. The only time she'd held a grudge for more than a day was when Drew, who was then eight, pantsed her in front of the horrible, mean neighbor kid. That had been seriously humiliating, and Jessica hadn't let Drew forget it. In fact, she could still to this day make him feel guilty just by saying, "Tommy. Underpants." (When she was in middle school, that was how she'd gotten a lot of her pocket money.)

Jessica began to pedal her bicycle more slowly as she neared Connor's house. She wanted to cool down — no sense in showing up on his doorstep sweating like a professional wrestler — but she was also nervous. Just because Lily had forgiven her abominable behavior didn't mean that Connor would. But all she could do was apologize, and then wait to see what he said.

She knocked on his door, and then tapped her feet apprehensively. A moment later, she knocked again. When, after five minutes, she was still standing on the front porch, eye to eye with a locked door, she decided there was nothing more to do but go home. She could call him, she supposed. Or maybe she should send a text: SO SRY. WANT 2 TALK 2 U ABT US. Yeah, right — that would totally work. Not.

As she was getting on her bike, she heard a noise behind her, and when she whirled around she saw Connor coming up the road wearing headphones and carrying his lacrosse stick under his arm.

She stood still as he approached but waved at him hesitantly.

"Hey," he said quietly, removing his headphones and resting his lacrosse stick against a birch tree.

"Doing a little practice for next season?" she asked. She hoped that if she just made a little small talk first, he'd give her the chance to apologize.

Connor shrugged noncommittally. "That, and working off a little aggression." The way he looked at her told her that she was to blame for said aggression.

Jessica nodded. So, the small talk avenue wasn't going to work for her. Well, there was always Plan B. Plan B went like this: grovel.

She reached for his hand, and she squeezed it as he let it lie lifelessly in her palm. "I came to apologize to you. I never, ever, ever should have jumped to that conclusion about you and Lily, and even if I had, I should have kept my big mouth shut." She paused, bit her lip, and then continued. "I don't want it to sound like I blame my cousin Greer, because I don't. But I think her whole inability to trust guys might be a little contagious." She grinned ruefully. "According to Greer, no guy is ever truly capable of staying loyal when there's a willing girl around . . ."

"I am," Connor said, his voice grave.

"I know," Jessica replied. "I know. I mean, I saw that firsthand! Because it seemed really weird to me when we agreed that we were going to . . . you know, sleep together, and then when I tried, you made it seem like you didn't want to. And so when I saw you with Lily, I guess I just thought to myself, 'Oh! That's why he won't sleep with me. Because he already has someone.'"

Connor shook his head as if he were disappointed in her. "Jess," he said, and his hand tightened around hers, "you should have known that I would never do something like that to you. When I told you I loved you, I meant it."

She looked up into his gray eyes. He'd used the past tense: He'd *meant* it. But how did he feel now? She took a deep breath. "Do you still mean it?"

He glanced away from her toward the water, as if he were looking for the answer in the ocean. Jessica held her breath and waited for what seemed like an eternity.

She felt a lump rising in her throat. If he didn't tell her what she wanted to hear in the next five seconds, she was going to turn into a weeping, trembling mess.

Connor pulled his hand away from hers and her heart sank. But then she felt his hands on her shoulders, and they were pulling her close.

"I still mean it," he said into her hair.

She felt the sob come up anyway, but it was one of gratitude rather than sorrow. She pressed into the comforting warmth of his chest, smelling laundry detergent and sunscreen and the faintest tang of sweat.

"I'm so sorry I didn't trust you," she whispered.

"And I'm sorry I didn't tell you what was going on. But Lily wanted me to keep it a secret, and it was such a big deal that I pretty much didn't have a choice."

She felt him kiss the top of her head, and then she lifted her face so he could kiss that, too.

"I missed you," she said. "Even thought it was only, like, a week."

Connor laughed. "It was even less than that."

She pulled back and gave him a tiny, playful shove. "Whatever. It felt like forever." She reached up and brushed the shaggy blondish brown bangs away from his lovely steel gray eyes. "And I'm leaving soon to go back to Ithaca, and I don't want to waste another minute of the time left. I want to spend it with you."

Grinning, Connor took her hand again. "How about we go on another date tonight," he suggested. "We can do the whole linen napkin and too many forks thing."

"Or," Jessica countered, squeezing his fingers between hers, "we can just make some sandwiches and eat them on the beach while the sun sets and the stars come out." She smiled. "You know I make *awesome* panini."

"Isn't that just a fancy word for grilled ham and turkey?" he teased.

"Whatever! Like you're so great in a kitchen, Mr. How Do I Make Toast Again?"

And then they both burst out laughing, and they laughed until they could hardly breathe. It was relief, Jessica thought, that made them cackle like a pair of hyenas. They were both just glad to be together again.

As she walked Connor to his door, she leaned her head

on his shoulder. There was something else she had to tell him. "That whole virginity thing?" she asked. "Maybe we should wait."

"I think so, too," he replied quietly. "We have lots of time."

Jessica pulled him to a halt before the porch. "I want to be clear about something, though," she said. "I still expect a lot of kissing. And I mean a *lot*."

Smiling, Connor bent down to her, and as his lips met hers hungrily, Jessica felt tiny jolts of pleasure in every part of her body. *Now, that's more like it*, she thought, and then for a long time she didn't think anything else.

"Your legs are, like, twice as long as mine," Lara declared, as Greer settled beside her in the hammock. "I mean, look at that. I'm, like, some kind of dwarf next to you." The hammock swayed beneath them as Greer stretched out a long tan calf and inspected it carefully.

"True," Greer mused, "my legs are longer. But you have much better ankles than I do. See how nice and delicate they are?"

"Ankles," Lara sighed. "Who cares about ankles?"

"Casting agents for foot models," Greer declared. "You could totally be a foot model."

Lara laughed. "You're insane."

For a while they were quiet, just resting in the giant hammock beneath their bedroom window. In the trees above them they could hear the twitter of tiny birds. ("I love those little black-and-white chickadees," Greer had said fondly. "They're so much nicer than the nasty Park Avenue pigeons.")

Lara was feeling philosophical. Sadness from her conversations with Drew and Marco lingered, but the more she thought about what had happened, the more she knew that it was for the best. Marco would be a sweet memory. And as far as Drew went, well, they lived in different states — different *worlds* — and they owed it to themselves to belong to the places they were in. She'd be able to go back to Chicago with her mom and Mike and enjoy herself without obsessing about the next plane to Ithaca. And that would be nice. And if, in the future, they decided they wanted to be together again, they could do that. But for now they would be good, loyal friends.

Lara sighed pensively. Soon they'd all be leaving, going their separate directions. Already the aunts were packing suitcases and making huge meals in an attempt to clear out the cupboards and the refrigerators. And already the uncles were sneaking out of the house at five A.M. to get in as much fishing as possible before they had to go back to their offices and carpools and Rotary Club meetings.

Lara was starting to feel ready to go herself. School would be starting soon, and she was going to take an awesome photography class. But in order to feel truly prepared to leave, she needed to talk to Jessica and make things right.

"Do you think if I clapped my hands, I could magically summon a servant to bring me an iced tea?" Greer's voice interrupted Lara's thoughts.

Lara smiled faintly. "Last I looked, the Tuttles weren't employing domestic help."

"Aunt Clare should totally hire someone next summer," Greer remarked. "Lord knows my mother is incapable of assistance. She doesn't even know how to turn on the oven and she has definitely never picked up a broom."

Next summer, Lara thought wistfully. "So do you think you'll be back?"

Greer shrugged. "Sure, why not?" She tried to seem blasé about it, but Lara knew she was dying to come back to Pebble Beach — mostly because of one handsome tennis coach named Hunter Brown.

"Assuming my mom and your uncle Mike stay married," Lara offered, "we'll be back, too. I mean, they're, like, two kids in love right now, but you know my mom's track record. I lost count of the marriages . . ."

Greer tried to flop over onto her stomach and the hammock started to wobble dangerously. Lara gripped the sides until Greer decided to remain where she was.

"Well," Greer said, "my mom only had one marriage, but as you know, that one went up in a giant ball of flames.

Oh, and did I tell you I got a message from my dad? He's in Cannes right now with two girlfriends. That's right: *two*." She sighed. "Talk about midlife crisis. Pretty soon he's going to call me and tell me he's getting a face-lift and calf implants."

Lara laughed; Greer's jaded outlook was eternally a source of amusement. She was the opposite of Jessica, who always looked on the bright side of everything.

But where was that girl? Lara wanted to know. She was just about to ask Greer to send her a text when she saw Jessica walking toward them, swinging her arms jauntily and looking not nearly as pissed off as when Lara last saw her.

"Hey," Greer called out. "Come join us."

Lara elbowed her in the ribs. Jessica might not be furious still, but they couldn't act as if nothing had happened. The fact was, both Lara and Greer had acted badly.

"Hi, Jess," Lara said softly.

Jessica stood over them with an unreadable expression on her face. Her hair was windblown and sun-bleached, and she looked beautiful and almost feral with her bare feet and tangled locks.

Lara struggled to sit up in the hammock. "Listen," she said, speaking quickly. She wanted to get it all out there before Jessica had a chance to rediscover her anger. "I want to apologize. I should have told you what was going on. I should have trusted that our relationship was strong enough to handle my problems with Drew. I'm really, really sorry, Jessica. And I promise to be honest with you from now on."

Then she elbowed Greer again. "I'm sorry, too," Greer piped up, as if on command. "It was totally uncool of me to keep secrets from you." She smiled her high-wattage smile, the one that Jessica used to call her "Magical Charm Ray." "Even though it was all Lara's fault."

This time, Lara poked Greer so hard in the ribs that she squealed. "Kidding! God!" she cried, laughing.

Lara looked up at Jessica to see a smile slowly spreading across her face. "I had to do my share of apologizing today, too," Jessica admitted. "And it went okay. Lily forgave me for outing her to her parents. And she told me . . . that Connor's not the baby's father. He was just being a good friend."

"Really?" Greer gasped, her eyes widening. "Oh, wow. That changes everything."

Jessica nodded, blushing. "It does. And I talked to Connor afterward, and he . . . well, he still loves me. And we decided we're both okay with waiting."

"So all's well," Lara declared.

Jessica looked closely at her two cousins. "If Connor and Lily can both forgive me, then who am I to hold a grudge? I forgive you both."

"Hooray!" Lara cried, and the next thing she knew, she and Greer were pulling Jessica onto the hammock. The hammock began to sway dangerously, which prompted the girls to all shriek with fear and glee. Their arms and legs were all tangled together, and Lara felt sure that any second, the hammock would flip and dump them all onto their butts. Luckily, she thought, the ground was covered in pine needles to cushion their falls.

But miraculously, the hammock steadied, and Jessica found her place on it, right between Lara and Greer. The three girls lay side by side, gazing up into the leaves.

"You know," Greer reflected, "I'm the only one who achieved my goal this summer." She paused, then went on, humor in her voice. "Not to rub it in or anything."

Lara yawned. The warmth and the breeze were making her sleepy. "Whatever happened to that list anyway?"

"You had better know where it is, Greer Hallsey," Jessica warned. "I told you if my mom ever found it, I would kill you, and I meant it. *I am very skilled with a lacrosse stick.*"

"Oh, you can relax," Greer assured her. "I know exactly where it is."

"It's ironic," Lara said thoughtfully. "My goal was to keep fewer secrets and I ended up keeping more." Realizing that didn't make her feel that great, but what could she do about it now? It was all water under the proverbial bridge.

"And Connor and I realized some pretty unwelcome consequences of losing your virginity!" Jessica laughed.

Greer stretched out her impossibly long legs and sighed. "Like I said, ladies, I'm the only one who can put a check mark through her goal." Then she grinned. "Oh, am I rubbing it in? Sorry."

Lara poked her yet again: The girl was going to have *bruises*. Lara thought back to the first day they'd arrived and what she'd said to them as they sat on Greer's bed. She decided to say it again. "Well," she said brightly, "next summer will be different."

"Wow," Greer exclaimed. "Where have I heard that before?"

And the three girls burst into laughter yet again, scaring the flock of chickadees from their perch.

"Hey, Greer," Jessica said. "Out of curiosity, where is the list?"

Greer yawned in mock boredom. "It's folded up in my drawer, inside a perfume box, right next to my silk pajamas. As I've told you a thousand times, I am excellent at keeping secrets secret."

Jessica launched herself out of the hammock. "I'll be right back," she cried as the other two girls looked after her in bafflement.

A few moments later, Jessica reappeared with the list of their summer goals in one hand and one of their room's many aromatherapy candles in another. Lara watched as Jessica placed the candle carefully on a stump, then lit it with a kitchen match.

As the flame flickered, sputtered, and gathered strength, Jessica held out the paper to Greer. "Would you like to do the honors?" she asked.

Greer grinned and accepted the paper, which was somewhat crumpled and torn from being carried in her purse and then stuffed into a box. "Well, ladies," she said, dangling the paper over the candle. "It's good-bye to summer, and good-bye to our goals."

The edge of the paper caught fire and turned black, and the small flame rose higher as it devoured the hopes they'd written down back in June.

Lara watched as Greer held the paper for a few more seconds, then let it drop to the ground where it burned to ashes and then quietly went out. "All my dreams, up in smoke!" she cried dramatically, holding her hand to her forehead like a 1940s Hollywood ingenue.

Greer and Jessica laughed, and then Lara joined in. "Maybe next year I'll pick an easier goal to meet," she said. "Like 'Get really tan.'"

Greer snorted. "I doubt you could do that, either," she teased. "It's August, and you're like Casper the Friendly Ghost over here."

Lara poked her cousin in the ribs one final time. "I'll just steal all your self-tanner, then."

"Sounds like a plan," Greer responded mildly. "I'll bring extra bottles."

Then Jessica put her arms around both her cousins. "I can't wait for next summer," she said.

And Lara had to smile. She was already looking forward to next summer, too.

To Do List:
Read all the Point books!

♡ 📖 ♡

Airhead
Being Nikki
Runaway
By **Meg Cabot**

Wish
By **Alexandra Bullen**

Suite Scarlett
Scarlett Fever
By **Maureen Johnson**

Sea Change
The Year My Sister Got Lucky
South Beach
French Kiss
Hollywood Hills
By **Aimee Friedman**

Ruined
By **Paula Morris**

Possessed
By **Kate Cann**

Top 8
By **Katie Finn**

And Then
Everything Unraveled
And Then I Found
Out the Truth
By **Jennifer Sturman**

Wherever Nina Lies
By **Lynn Weingarten**

Girls In Love
Summer Girls
Summer Boys
Next Summer
After Summer
Last Summer
By **Hailey Abbott**